JUSTICE ONLY SLEPT

A Prof. Will Hampton Novel

William A. Edwards

ISBN: 198437494X
ISBN 13: 9781984374943
Library of Congress Control Number: 2018901708
CreateSpace Independent Publishing Platform
North Charleston, South Carolina

Justice hath not been dead, though it hath slept,

Shakespeare, Measure For Measure

For Wanda, Thank you, Thank you very very much

CHAPTER ONE

"Dr. Hampton, this is Sarah Brinkman, Dr. Walter Kelly's secretary at Georgia Tech. Walter is out of town—speaking at a conference—but I just got a call from T. Edward Troutman, senior partner of the large downtown Atlanta law firm that represents the local Boy Scout Council as well as the insurance company that insures the Council. There has been an explosion in a cave in North Georgia. Two Scouts and a Scoutmaster are dead. Mr. Troutman wanted Walter to go up there as soon as possible and perhaps shed some light on what might have happened. I explained to Mr. Troutman that Walter is out of town but I also told him that I knew who Walter would want me to call under the circumstances. He said to make the call. Can and will you call Mr. Troutman right now and then head to Caseville, Georgia, right away?"

"Sure. Right now. What's Mr. Troutman's phone number."

"Here it is, and one other thing—Mr. Troutman always pays well for consultations and pays promptly. You owe me dinner, Professor."

"You have a deal, Sarah. And thanks for calling me."

Will Hampton and Walter Kelly had been roommates as undergraduates at The Citadel. Walter had majored in Physics while Will majored in Biology and Chemistry. Both had earned PhDs albeit from different universities but had renewed their friendship now that Walter was at Georgia Tech in Atlanta and Will was teaching nearby at Emory at Oxford.

Will immediately telephoned Mr. Troutman, who answered on the first ring.

"Dr. Hampton, Ms. Brinkman tells me that, next to her boss—Dr. Walter Kelly—you are perhaps the brightest mind in Georgia."

"Mr. Troutman, she is being far too generous, but I'll be glad to help you if I can. If I don't think I am who you need, I'll try to recommend someone."

"Dr. Hampton, two Boy Scouts and their Scoutmaster are dead in Waterfall Cave in northwest Georgia near Caseville. Our law firm represents both The Atlanta Area Council Boy Scouts of America as well as the insurance company that insures the Council. There was an explosion in the cave. That is all we know at this point. We need someone up there immediately to find out what happened and to be our eyes and ears on the ground."

"Mr. Troutman, I know that cave well. I have been in it several times. I grew up in Northside Atlanta and was in Scouts. In fact, I am an Eagle and our troop explored that cave several times. It's on Sanders Road going northwest out of Caseville."

"Professor Hampton, you are obviously far better suited to help us than I could have ever hoped for. Since you know the cave, you will not have to waste any time exploring it or having its layout explained to you. I also need to let you know that this tragedy has a very sensitive aspect. The Scout troop involved is not from Northside Atlanta. It is from Southside Atlanta. It is a Negro troop. At this point, we must consider the possibility that whatever happened was directed against that particular group. Two FBI agents, Dick Harrison and Martin Roberts, are just now leaving Atlanta in route to Caseville to observe. They are both experienced and first-rate agents in the Atlanta office."

"Actually, Mr. Troutman, I know both men. We all attended the same church in Buckhead when I was growing up. In fact, I even had a few dates with Mr. Harrison's daughter before she and I went off to college."

"Professor, that is even better. You will just be an unofficial observer but try to find out what actually happened, and then get to a phone and call me back collect, day or night. Let me give you my home number as well as this direct line into my office. If I don't answer my office phone, tell my secretary who you are. She will know where to find me immediately. Once again, thank you for stepping in with no advance notice. Needless to say, we will pay you as a consultant and cover your expenses."

CHAPTER TWO

Timing could not have been more propitious for Will. He had just completed grading his final exams from fall semester, posted the grades and forwarded them to the registrar. He taught both biology and chemistry in the small, elite two-year college in Oxford, Georgia, just outside Atlanta. It was the original home of Emory University and funneled many of its best students into Emory upon their successfully completing two years at Oxford. When Sarah Brinkman's call came, he was mulling over options for Christmas break. This was to be his first real vacation since he started teaching three years ago in the fall of 1958. Heretofore, every holiday had been spent preparing for the next semester's classes. But now, he had taught all of next semester's classes twice, and he could tweak his notes each week from last year's classes through the upcoming semester as he went along.

He had been thinking New Orleans for the holidays. He had friends from college who were always inviting him down and offering a place to stay, plus guaranteeing him plenty of good food, good music and this time probably the 1961 Sugar Bowl, Arkansas vs Alabama. However, now it looked like Caseville, Georgia, was to be his holiday.

Caseville was about an hour and half northwest of Atlanta and in the northwest corner of Georgia just below Chattanooga, Tennessee. During the Civil War, there had been heavy fighting at nearby Lookout Mountain and Chickamauga Creek. Waterfall Cave had actually played a small role in those battles. Confederate troops had harvested bat guano from the cave and used its high nitrogen content to manufacture much needed gunpowder. In fact, that work had made Waterfall Cave much more accessible to later cave explorers. Upon entering the cave it forked right and left. Its right fork would have required substantial crawling because the roof was only a foot or so above the floor. However, Confederate troops had dug a trench in the floor, thus allowing access through the low ceiling area with only minimal bending over. Once through the low ceiling area the cave opened up with large rooms and massive formations. It was known among Scout Troops as a spectacular beginner's cave.

CHAPTER THREE

Will immediately left his office in Science Hall and headed to Carriage House on the grounds of Braxton Hall where he lived. Braxton Hall was an estate near the college presently owned and occupied by the widow of P.T.F. Calhoun, deceased president of Oxford Bank. Will would not have been able to afford the rent on even this carriage house except for the fact that he maintained the grounds for P.T.F.'s, widow who now owned and occupied the estate. Within a few short minutes of leaving Science Hall, Will was home, had thrown together some clothes and camping gear into the trunk of his car, and headed for Caseville, Georgia.

Once in Caseville, he drove around the town square with the courthouse situated in the center and then out the west side of town on Old Sanders Road. About a mile or so above the cave entrance, Will pulled into an old gas station and parked alongside several other cars already parked there. The station was closed—probably because of activity down at the cave—and Will left his car there, electing to walk the remaining mile or so down to the cave entrance. He knew that there would not be much room for vehicles at cave entrance. There wasn't much room when nothing was happening but, with the situation in the cave, it would be a three-ring circus today. And even though Old Sanders Road was surfaced, it was hardly wide enough for two cars to pass each other.

As Will had expected, sheriff's cars were parked all around the front of the cave entrance and completely blocked the road. The actual cave entrance, about 20 yards off the road, was about five feet high and fifteen feet wide.

Deputies and Georgia State Troopers stood conferring at the entrance. Will spotted Dick Harrison and Martin Roberts about the same time as they spotted him. They moved around the edge of the crowd toward each other. Will immediately began explaining why he was there, but it was quickly apparent that he was expected.

Roberts explained, "At this point we have no idea what caused the explosion in the cave. The boys were using carbide lamps as a light source. Their flames must have ignited something. Now we are waiting for the National Guard or a fire department unit from Chattanooga to get here with breathing apparatus so the cave can be entered safely and the bodies recovered."

"How many were involved and where are the survivors now?" Will asked

"As best we can tell," Roberts continued, "there were about a dozen in the group, two Scoutmasters and ten Scouts. One Scoutmaster and two Scouts were killed. Those killed are still in the cave. The survivors are downtown at the Baptist Church in Caseville. People in Caseville have rallied and are doing all that they can to be helpful. Once word of the tragedy got out, the entire town turned out and gathered at the church."

"Do you think I could talk to the surviving Scoutmaster?" Will asked.

"You can try," Roberts replied. "I'll go with you. Don't know if it will help open any doors for you. Dick and I have already met him briefly and he knows why we are here. Dick can stay here and keep tabs on whatever happens while we are down at the church."

CHAPTER FOUR

Caseville Baptist Church was easy to find. It was the largest building in Caseville, and it was located just off the town square on the most prominent lot in town. The entire congregation and most of Caseville had turned out to support victims of the explosion and their families. Even townspeople of other denominations were there supporting the Baptists. Tables had been set up in Fellowship Hall and were now loaded with every kind of food imaginable and plenty of it. As victims' parents arrived, they were invited to get plates and eat as much as they desired. If they simply wanted a quiet place to await developments from the cave, the sanctuary was open and available to them. The surviving Scouts were in the Pastor's private conference room.

Will and Roberts entered Fellowship Hall. It was easy to spot the surviving Scoutmaster. He was in uniform talking with a group of parents. When Roberts motioned to him, he immediately left the group and came over to where Roberts and Will stood.

Roberts started the introductions. "Will, this is L.T. Jackson, Scoutmaster of the troop in the cave. He was with the troop and in the cave when the explosion took place. Mr. Jackson, this is Dr. Will Hampton. Will is a professor at Oxford College and is here at the request of the Council. It may interest you to know that he grew up in the church I attend in Atlanta and that he was in the Scouting program there. In fact, he is an Eagle Scout. We are trying to sort out what happened. Would you mind answering some questions for Will? We won't keep you long, I promise."

"I'll tell you everything I know, but I don't think I know very much," Jackson started. "When you go in the cave, it quickly forks to the right and to the left. We took the left fork and followed it way on back in. It is an easy walk because you can stand up all the way. You kind of have to watch your step toward the end because a small underground stream sort of follows and runs alongside the pathway. At the end, there is a large chamber. It is about twenty yards across. At the edge of the chamber, it drops down into a pit that is probably ten or fifteen feet deep. But on the far side of the pit, a rockslide goes up almost to the ceiling of the chamber. Right at the top there is a small opening to the outside. Several of the boys dropped down into the pit and then climbed up the other side. One of them stuck his head out of the opening to the outside, and then pulled back in real quick. He said it opened up into the backyard of someone's house and that the owner yelled at him to stay off his property. They came back through the pit. We dropped them a rope that they used to climb out of the pit. At that point we turned around and headed back to the entrance.

"Someone had dug trenches through the low parts of the other fork. Otherwise, we would have had to crawl through some pretty tight and muddy passages. At the end though, it was worth it. There is a huge room. It is probably bigger than this church. We just sat down on a large rock and stared in amazement. Finally, we turned around and headed back to the entrance. Our carbide lamps were starting to run a little low.

"All I just told you about happened yesterday. We left the cave, went up to Cloudland Canyon State Park, and camped out last night. It got down near freezing last night so the boys were up at the crack of dawn building fires and trying to get warm. Most of our gear is primitive. Some are lucky enough to have Army surplus, but most of us don't. We just sort of toughed it out with blankets.

"Anyway, after cleaning up from breakfast we still had plenty of time before we had to head back to Atlanta. Literally all of the boys wanted to go back in the cave and repel down into the pit and play around on ropes and that is what we intended to do. We got to the cave, reloaded our carbide lamps and started through the left fork. We had just gotten to the edge of the pit. Scoutmaster Johnson was leading. I was bringing up the rear.

"I heard someone say 'I smell gasoline,' and then there was an explosion. I ran to the front of the line. The two Scouts who had been at the front were lying at the bottom of the pit. George, the other Scoutmaster, jumped down into the pit to help them. Then he fell over and did not move again. I turned all of the other Scouts around and got them out of the cave as fast as I could. As soon as we got out of the cave, I put one of the older boys in charge and told everyone to stay out of the cave no matter what. Going back in would only make matters worse. There was nothing we could do to help those still in the cave. I got in my car, drove down to the sheriff's office to get help, and then immediately drove back to the cave. Deputy Sheriffs followed me back down to the cave. We loaded up all of the boys and brought them down here to the church. I called the emergency number for the Area Council Office and reported what had happened. They took it from there. I have wondered if the property owner of the property that has the little hole in his back yard may have poured gasoline down the hole to run us off. I haven't mentioned that to anyone yet. I don't know who is related to who around here or how some may feel about us being up here. That's about it as best I know."

"Mr. Jackson," Will said, "I know exactly what you are talking about. Our Troop went into Waterfall Cave several times. It was always great fun even in winter because, as you know, it's a pretty comfortable, 50-or-so degrees inside the cave even if it is zero degrees outside. In fact, we had to break away icicles one time to get in the cave. But tell me about the explosion. Did you ever smell gasoline?"

"I think so. I don't think it is my imagination. Just as I was about to enter the pit area, I kind of lost my footing on the slippery path and one foot slipped into the tiny creek that runs along the path. That is when I think I got a whiff of gasoline. Johnson had just started saying that he smelled gasoline."

Will then asked Jackson if he had noticed any kind of a sheen on the creek.

"No, not that I can remember. It all happened so fast. I was walking down the path looking straight ahead and, as one foot slid off of the path and into the tiny creek, I think I got a whiff of gasoline and everything exploded."

"Mr. Jackson, you are very correct about the victims in the pit," Will said. "They could not have been saved without their rescuers becoming victims too. The parents of the other eight boys owe you a great debt for getting their boys out as quickly as you did. There may have already been other explosions or there might be more at any time. Thank you for your time and thank you for your service to Scouting. One of these days you will have a better idea of how many lives you influenced in a positive way."

After Roberts and Will were outside of the church, Roberts stopped Will and asked, "What are you thinking, Professor?"

Will looked at Roberts for a moment. "First of all, I am all but positive that the property owner at the rabbit hole had nothing to do with anything. We are not dealing with a crime here. A terrible tragedy, yes. An intentional malicious act, no."

"What the hell, Will. If there was gasoline in the cave this morning but not yesterday, how did it get there and where did it come from? Why today but nothing yesterday?"

"Mr. Roberts, I can't answer all of your questions quite yet, but I think I know where to start looking. I am pretty sure that the presence of gasoline today and its absence yesterday is an accident of timing. A terrible accident, yes, but an accident nonetheless. Let's head back to the cave. Drop me off at where I parked my car and if you can, get the Sheriff and bring him back up to where I'm parked with as little fanfare as possible."

Moments later, after dropping Will at his car, Roberts returned with the Sheriff and Dick Harrison. Roberts made introductions all around and then turned to Will and said, "OK, Will, front and center. What's going on?"

"First," Will started explaining, "I can't prove anything at this point. But I think gasoline is leaking from one of the underground gasoline storage tanks at this gas station, into the ground water and flowing down into the cave. It just started getting into the cave this morning or perhaps last night. That is why there was no problem when the Scouts were in the cave yesterday. How can we prove it? Let's get the station owner down here and open up the tank caps. Then we can add dye to each tank. We will add a different color to each tank. That way we will know which tank is leaking. Sheriff, I'm sure you know the station owner. Do you think he will work with us on this?"

"I'm sure he will. He is a fine man. He is probably over at Caseville Baptist right now. Of course, he has no idea about what you think may have happen. He will be horrified. I'll go get him and let you explain it to him. He will be just as shocked as I am."

He then turned to Roberts and asked, "Martin, can you run me back down the hill to the cave? My car is down there."

Will then asked the Sheriff to send one of his deputies up to the gasoline station where they were assembled. "If I'm right, and I'm pretty sure I am, we need to implement some safety precautions right now. Your deputy and I can start working on those while you are gone."

In less than five minutes, the Sheriff's car passed by headed back up the hill into town and a deputy sheriff drove up and got out of his car. "Hi. I'm Tom Marlow. What's going on? Sheriff just said for me to get over here without saying anything to anybody and do anything and everything you guys told me to do. So, here I am. Tell me what to do."

Will quickly explained that they thought gasoline was leaking from the underground storage tanks at the station where they were standing and that it was leaking into the ground water and flowing into the cave.

"We need to get everyone away from the area around the cave. We don't know how fast gasoline is leaking into the cave. Any spark might set off another explosion if the critical amount of gasoline and air accumulate and mix with each other in the cave since the last explosion," Will explained.

"Then we need to seal off this road both above and below the cave entrance. Only those absolutely necessary can go near the cave and as few of them as possible. They need to be made aware of the source of the danger and the risk that they face. And finally, we need to alert the property owner with the rabbit hole in his back yard. Gasoline vapor might rise up out from the pit area of the cave before we find the leak and cause another explosion from that end. Mr. Roberts, your thoughts?"

"Spoken like the learned professor you are, Will. Mr. Marlow, will you organize the other deputies and clear everyone off of the road and then set up blockades on the road well above and below the cave?"

"Will do." Marlow said and promptly got in his car and headed back to the cave.

Within a few minutes, cars started leaving the cave area and heading back up the hill toward town. Moments later, a county truck showed up, dropped off sawhorses to block the road, and then headed down the road to the other side of the cave.

Before Will could get comfortably situated in his car, the Sheriff and station owner arrived.

"Professor Hampton, this is Quinton Bell, owner of this station. He is 100% with us on this. Tell Professor Hampton what you have, Quinton."

"Professor Hampton, I have what I call long yardsticks. Of course, they are much longer than a yard. They reach all the way down to the storage tank bottom and stick out the top at the same time. We can check the wet mark on the stick and it will tell us how many inches of gasoline we have left in the tank. All I ever have to know is how many inches are left in the tank to know when to reorder. I even have some old dye packs somewhere. My wholesale distributor gave those to all of us retailers several years ago. I guess for just such an occasion like this."

Will started not to ask the next question but went ahead. "Mr. Bell, do you ever use your yard sticks to monitor the declining level of gasoline in the tanks? You know, record the levels and compare the levels to the amount of gasoline sold day by day?"

"No sir," Bell replied, "I run the station by myself and always have a pretty good idea when it is about time to reorder. When I think it is about time to reorder I just drop the stick down into the tank and see how many inches are left. Don't keep any records or anything."

Bell then left the group, opened up the station, and after rummaging around inside for a few minutes, returned holding two bags of powdered dye, one green, one red.

Will made no attempt to calculate the volume of gasoline in each tank. "What the hell," Will thought to himself and dumped an entire bag in each tank.

"Now we wait," he said. "Mr. Bell, do you think the kind folks back at Caseville Baptist would object to us poaching some of that wonderful food spread out in Fellowship Hall?"

"Please be my guest, Professor," Bell offered. "My wife did fried chicken and deviled the eggs. Just be careful what you say. Most folks around here are pretty proud of their cooking and could easily take serious offense if you even suggest that it's not the best you have ever had anywhere anytime, bar none."

CHAPTER FIVE

U pon arrival back at Caseville Baptist, Will saw Quinton Bell head straight to a clean cut young man in a group of locals. The young man looked at Will and headed straight over.

"Professor Hampton. I am Terry Rogers, pastor here at Caseville Baptist. Quinton was just telling me that you might have answered the question that has been on everyone's mind all day. I understand that you may not have conclusive proof yet, but let me just say that the possibility that it was intentional is weighing very heavy on the hearts of many people, both those who live here in Caseville and of course the Scouts and their parents. Like I said, I know you don't have proof yet, but would you just say something and let everyone know that you don't believe foul play was involved?"

"Right," Will said. "I know where you are coming from. And actually, we do have some proof that foul play was not involved. You see, Scoutmaster Jackson smelled gasoline when he stepped in the creek just this side of the pit. If gasoline had been thrown down into the pit from outside it would not have been in the creek up on this side of the pit."

Rev. Rogers promptly found a spoon and a glass of water. He tapped the glass with the spoon in the finest tradition of church gatherings everywhere and announced there was some important information everyone would be interested in hearing. He introduced Will and then stepped back. Will explained that he thought that the gasoline entered the cave through ground water flowing in that direction. He wasn't sure of the source of the gasoline yet but hoped to have some answers within the next day or so. In any event, it did not appear to him that any foul play of any kind was involved.

Will's comments were followed by applause. Scoutmaster Jackson came over to Will with tears in his eyes and gave Will a heartfelt hug. He was followed by another man Will had noticed but had not met yet.

"Professor, you have performed a great service. I am Ned Conway and I own the little farm that has the little 'rabbit hole' cave exit on it. Many people have been thinking that maybe I poured gasoline down into the cave. I didn't and never would have either. You have lifted a heavy burden from me. Thank you, sir. I hope that if I can ever do anything to repay you that you will let me. Thank you and God bless you, sir."

Will then asked Rev. Rogers if there was a telephone he could use to place a couple of collect phone calls. Rogers took Will to the church office and told him not to worry about any charges.

Will first called Edward Troutman and gave him a progress report. Will thought that more gasoline might make it into the cave by sometime tomorrow and if gasoline from the station was indeed the culprit, they should see the dye by then. After all, gasoline had not been in the cave Saturday but was on Sunday. Troutman told Will to take as much time as he needed. If he needed to go to Chattanooga to get a room for the night, by all means, do so.

Next, Will placed a collect call to Dean J.O. Herring at the college. Herring accepted the charges and immediately asked, "What the hell is going on lad? Edna Calhoun, your guardian angel and landlord, told my wife Eleanor this morning that you left out first thing this morning driving like a bat out of hell."

Will explained where he was and what he was doing and furthered explained that it might be a day or so before he got back to Oxford. Even when Will was technically on his own time, he always stayed in touch with Dean Herring. Over the two and a half years that Will had taught at the college, they had developed a very close personal friendship. Herring had initially interviewed Will when Will had applied for the job opening and recommended hiring him to the hiring committee. Since Will had arrived at Oxford, Herring and his wife had adopted him and even arranged for him to live in the carriage house at Braxton Hall. Edna Calhoun and Dean Herring's wife were best and lifelong friends.

Troutman's conversation had reminded Will that he needed to arrange for a place to spend the night. He didn't mind camping out at Cloudland Canyon State Park situated above Caseville. He had many times before and he had brought camping gear for that purpose. One thing was certain, though. He couldn't sleep in the cave as he had on some previous occasions. However, the more he thought about it, the more he thought it might be convenient to be closer to the cave and it certainly would be more comfortable in a motel. Indeed, a hot shower and warm bed would be a very welcome luxury particularly since he was on an expense account. However, right off hand, he could not remember any motels in or around Caseville, and he did not really want to go all of the way to Chattanooga.

Upon returning into Fellowship Hall, Will found that all three bodies had been removed from the cave and were ready to be transported to the State Crime Lab in Atlanta. Upon being notified, all the Scouts and their families formed up and started the sad trip back to Atlanta. FBI agents Dick Harrison and Martin Roberts agreed that only one of them needed to stay until the source of the gasoline in the cave was conclusively established. They flipped coins and Roberts stayed. Standing there looking at the array of food still left in Fellowship Hall, Will concluded that Roberts had won the toss. Roberts had quickly picked up a plate and started working the tables like an experienced southern churchgoer.

Ned Conway, owner of the farm above the cave, came over to where Will was standing and said "Professor, I can offer you a place to stay while you are here. My wife died two years ago. I have a large house with just me rattling around in it. My daughter lives away. She teaches school up in Chattanooga. She's a biology teacher like you, only she teaches in high school."

Will's protests fell on deaf ears. Conway continued to insist that Will accept his offer of hospitality. It was the least he could do since Will had cleared his name of any wrongdoing.

Will finally relented and then followed Conway as Conway headed back to the food-laden tables where he began preparing a to-go plate to eat later for supper. Will got the message and did likewise.

CHAPTER SIX

Conway's house was a beautiful stone house sitting atop a small hill with sloping yards running down in all directions. At the bottom of one slope was the small opening into Waterfall Cave. Beautiful though the house was, it was the contents that truly astounded Will. Immediately upon entering the house, Will saw turned wooden bowls. Large bowls. Small bowls and everything in between. Some were turned from walnut. Some from cherry. There was curly maple and a wood Will could not identify.

"Mr. Conway, you are obviously a master wood turner. I would love to see your shop."

Then the full impact of the contents of the house began to sink in. All of the wood furniture was handmade. Like the bowls, some was from walnut, some was from cherry, and some was from maple. There were even a few pieces made from mahogany. Most of the pieces were reproductions of beautiful period antiques from the late 18th century and early 19th century though a few were quite modern. All manifested the perfectly proportioned lines and curves of a master craftsman born with the eye for symmetry and beauty, and all manifested the execution of a master cabinetmaker.

"Mr. Conway, I apologize. You are much more than just a master wood turner. You are indeed a master craftsman. Your work is museum quality."

"Professor, I've been known to make a little saw dust from time to time. Actually, the bowls put my daughter through college. It's hard to make any kind of a living in this part of the country. There is very little farmable land. Too steep and too rocky. On top of that, the growing season is short. I managed to grow a little corn every year but by the time my crop came in, crops south of here had been in for weeks and the price had dropped to where a fellow could not make a profit. Like most of us around here, I ended up exporting my corn crop out of here in liquid form and in Mason jars. My dad worked himself to death cutting trees, dragging them out of the woods and hand hewing them into railroad ties, which he sold for 50 cents each. I've always done some logging. I started saving the really beautiful woods—the walnut, the cherry, the figured maple. Sawed it up and stowed it in my barn for it to air dry. Didn't have any particular plans for it. Just thought it was too nice to let get away.   My wife wanted a sewing table. I had the wood and could buy a used table saw cheaper than I could buy her a table. Bought the table saw and made her the table. After that, there was no turning back. She got a Williamsburg furniture catalog from somewhere and had me in the shop just about every waking hour.

"Somewhere along the way, I bought a pretty nice lathe and a set of turning tools from an estate down in Rome, Georgia. Started turning bowls and vases. Folks said I had an eye for it and I guess I did. Started going to county fairs and craft shows. Won some prizes and I started selling them. Like I said, they put my daughter through college, and they were a hell of a lot easier to make than corn liquor. Lot safer too. Never knew when your still might get cut down and you would get sent off courtesy of Uncle Sam when you were in the 'manufacturing business.' How about you, Professor? Not many folks would have even noticed my stuff. You jumped on it right off."

"Mr. Conway, like you, I make a little sawdust from time to time. My mother was an avid antiquer. When I was growing up, she drug me all over Atlanta looking at antiques in every antique shop in town. Eventually, I started seeing some that I liked, or, as you said, I began developing an eye for what was well made or well proportioned. Mom began collecting some southern pieces, which I inherited. She and my dad were killed in a plane crash when I was away at school. I'm an only child so I inherited everything.

"I haven't bought much. Can't afford the stuff I like on a teacher's salary. But I've been to Williamsburg, The Museum of Early Southern Decorative Arts in Winston-Salem and, of course, The Charleston Museum in Charleston, South Carolina. All three are great about letting visitors take pictures of furniture and to make measured drawings. Even some of the shops in Atlanta still recognize me and let me copy pieces for future reference. I make a few pieces along whenever I have time. Most of my tools belonged to my father. They are, of course, old but I think the pre-World War II tools are, by and large, better than the ones being made today. Anyway, I have a large folder of future projects."

"Professor, it is indeed a pleasure to make your acquaintance—you being a fellow woodworker and all. Let's eat some supper after which we can share some very fine homemade apple brandy."

After, supper, Conway and Will settled into comfortable overstuffed leather chairs in front of the fireplace in Conway's paneled den and Conway produced a Mason jar of fine old "handmade" brandy "held available only for special occasions."

Will kept looking at the paneling in the room but could not identify it. Finally, he asked Conway what kind of wood it was.

"Chestnut. Not surprising that you did not recognize it. It's pretty much all gone. Blight came through the early part of this century and killed off all of the trees. They were massive trees and very important. Their nuts fed animals as well as humans. As you can see, it has very straight grain and a nice color. I can remember working in my yard and hearing the dead trees crash down out in the nearby woods. Seemed like one would go down about every hour. They were the mainstay of our Southern forests."

"Are some of your turnings also from chestnut?" Will asked.

"They are. Hesitate selling them now. Just don't have much chestnut left. Back when they were falling down, I didn't realize what a treasure trove I had. Now it is almost too late. Professor, before you leave, I want you to pick out one of my chestnut turnings as my thank you for what you have done for me, and I want to give you a couple of chestnut blanks to turn when you get around to it. It would give me a lot of pleasure to know that you have one of my bowls. It's comforting when one goes to someone that I know really appreciates it."

Then, after an appropriate amount of pleasant conversation and wonderful brandy, Will was shown to a guest room off the den, and Conway headed down the hall to his bedroom.

Will had been asleep for an indeterminate period. At first, he thought he was dreaming. Perhaps the brandy was working wonders. It seemed that there was a warm naked female body next to his and her hand was easing down inside the front of his boxer shorts. Will quickly realized that he was not dreaming.

"What the hell?" Will was saying when the hand went up over his mouth and young woman's voice whispered, "Quiet! If you wake up my dad, he will kill both of us."

Instantly, her hand was back inside the front of his boxer shorts and was again very skillfully manipulating him.

"You can't do this," Will whispered.

"Be quiet and be still," she whispered. "We can and we are."

Her hand went to her mouth and brought moisture down on Will. Then she eased over on top of Will and put him inside of her.

In due time, she moved off Will and moved over next to him as close as she could get. "Now that wasn't too bad, was it? Put your arms around me and hold me for a few minutes. And thank you very much even though you were, shall we say, something less than very enthusiastic. And now you can go back to sleep, Dr. Hampton."

Will was still trying to get his thoughts together somewhat later when once again the hand went into the front of his boxers. In spite of his best efforts, Will rose to the occasion. This time she reached down, pulled his boxers down out of the way, and gently took Will briefly into her mouth. Then she again rolled over on top of him and put him inside of her, once again making what Shakespeare described as the beast with two backs.

Will was a much more active participant this time, and after both were completely satisfied, he gathered her into his arms and drew her close. Within a few minutes, though, she eased out of the bed whispering to Will, "I must go. Thank you very very much. If I stay any longer, I will only get more warm and comfortable, fall asleep and then my Dad will catch us in the morning. He will be up at the crack of dawn. You'll see." Then, without another sound, she was gone.

Will thought about trying to follow her but he had no idea where she was in the house or, perhaps more importantly, where her father was.

CHAPTER SEVEN

Sunlight was streaming through his bedroom windows when Will finally woke up. As he got out of bed and headed to the bathroom, he noticed a pair of panties on the floor next to his bed. It hadn't been a dream. It had obviously been Conway's daughter, but what the hell. He picked them up and put them in his rucksack.

After showering and dressing, Will crossed though the den to the kitchen where he found Conway frying country ham and pulling biscuits out of the oven. Red eye gravy, cheese grits and eggs quickly followed. As they sat down at the kitchen table, a tall, slender and very attractive young woman—maybe ten years older than Will—walked into the kitchen, kissed Conway on the top of his head and poured herself a cup of coffee.

"Connie, didn't know you were in. When did you get here, my dear?" Conway asked.

"Came in late last night. Saw all of the commotion on TV late yesterday afternoon. Looked like a lot of folks thought you might have had something to do with the explosion in the cave, but then somebody figured out what really happened and saved your hide."

"Honey, this is Professor Will Hampton from Oxford College. He is the one who, as you just said, figured out what really happened and saved my hide."

"Then, Professor, we are very much indebted to you. I wish that there was something we could do to at least partially repay you for saving my father's reputation and perhaps his hide."

Will was pretty sure he caught glimpse of a very subtle wink from the girl.

"Certainly, the hospitality of this house is more than adequate payment," Will said watching Conway and at the same time trying to read Connie's expression.

Conway got up and began clearing the dishes from the table. As he walked away from the table, his daughter threw Will a silent kiss. Will winked back.

Then Will said to no one in particular, "I need to go down to the cave and see if any dye has started coming through."

Conway said he definitely wanted to go, and Connie asked what they were talking about. Will briefly explained his theory of the origin of the gasoline in the cave. He then gathered up his gear and headed for the door.

Will stowed his gear in the trunk of his car, which was a little British racing green 1952 MG TD sports car. Connie stood there admiring the little car and then ask if she could ride down to the cave with him. Without waiting for an answer, she climbed in and sat waiting for Will.

Will climbed into the car and, as he started the engine, turned to Connie and said, "You certainly know how to thank a fellow for a perceived favor."

"I would thank you, again, right here and right now, except that it would undoubtedly get us both killed. But sometime soon and some place, you must let me again show you my appreciation. And sometime and some place very soon."

CHAPTER EIGHT

Once at the cave, they could detect the faint odor of gasoline in the ground water trickling into the cave. However, there was no sign of any coloration in the water.

Conway announced that he was going down town to Adam's Cafe for coffee and the latest gossip and invited Will to join him. He also offered Will use of the house while monitoring the cave throughout the day.

After Conway left, Will opted to go back to the warm house. Connie asked for a ride back up to the house so she could get her car and head back to Chattanooga.

When they got back up to the house, Will had not even gotten his jacket off before Connie had her arms around his neck and her lips firmly planted on his.

"I'm not wearing any panties," Connie said.

"I know," Will replied. "And I know where they are. But you won't be needing them for a little while because now ...."

They were quickly back in Will's bed, moving closer and closer to each other, legs entwined, fingers exploring, lips caressing and then both bodies completely joined followed by mutual release.

Somewhat later, after an encore, Connie did head back to Chattanooga and Will continued to monitor the cave. Roberts was also keeping a watchful eye on the cave by then and was beginning to worry whether Will's theory was in fact correct. Then, late that afternoon, wisps of red dye began to appear in the water indicating gasoline leaking into the cave, much to the relief of everyone.

Will went to the church office and once again called Edward Troutman—this time with the report that dyed gasoline had appeared in the cave's ground water. Troutman requested a written report from Will as soon as possible and again promised a consultation fee, only this time he promised a generous fee in view of Will's splendid work. Will then headed to the church's Fellowship Hall in search of food but where, much to his amazement, TV crews were interviewing Roberts and assorted locals. Will attempted to escape, but as soon as he was seen, a cheer went up from the crowd and TV crews immediately surrounded him. Ultimately, giving up on having a shot at the food tables, he eased out a side door and made it to his car.

Driving back home he thought constantly about both Conway and his daughter. He would like to see more of them both. He was wondering if he could get Conway to part with a few more pieces of chestnut so he might turn a set of bowls. Certainly, the chestnut vase Conway had let him select was just perfect. It was perfectly shaped like a Chinese vase.

CHAPTER NINE

It had been well after dark when Will at last got home from Caseville. First thing the next morning, he went to his office in Science Hall and wrote, and then mailed his report to Mr. Troutman. Then as he turned to the most pressing problem at hand, what to do over the holidays and where to do it, there were three quick raps on his office door and Dr. J.O. Herring, Dean of the College, stepped inside.

"Will, my boy, Eleanor and I were talking about you last night after watching all of the news coverage from up in Caseville. Great job by the way. Great job. Good for the college too. We are worried about you, though. There is no frivolity in your life. Doesn't look like there ever has been. You did four years at The Citadel, and then went straight through grad school. You've been teaching here two years now plus one semester. But what have you ever done just for the hell of it? Loosen up, lad. Get out. Make some new friends. Meet some young women. Hell, get laid. Leave our coeds alone, of course, and I admit that there is not anything of interest on our faculty. But, with all that will be going on in Atlanta over the holidays, turn Eleanor loose and she will have you booked up morning, noon and night, especially after you were talked about on every TV station in Georgia, middle Tennessee and northeast Alabama. It will make you a happier person and even a lot more fun to be around."

Will had been hearing that advice most of his adult life. "You're right J.O. My parents used to say I turned 50 on my 12th birthday. But before we turn Eleanor loose, let me look into a couple of things I've been thinking about. If I don't come up with something that doesn't involve a textbook or a lab manual, then we can call in Eleanor."

CHAPTER TEN

Will ended up in New Orleans for the holidays. Stayed with his friends from college. Ate fantastic food. Listened to wonderful music. Partied constantly. Even went to the Sugar Bowl where Alabama beat Arkansas 10 to 2. Bear Bryant's Tide was just too much for Frank Broyles' Razorbacks. Will didn't get laid but it was a wonderful end to 1961 nevertheless.

There was a time in this country when there were no Interstate Highways. Then highways went through every town. They passed every restaurant, motel, dive and juke joint between point A and point B. Will was driving back home from New Orleans and was somewhere past Montgomery and heading toward Atlanta, thinking that he might even push all of the way home that night.

He rounded a bend and started down a long straight stretch of highway when suddenly the car behind him pulled out and pulled up beside him. They flipped on their interior lights. It looked like there were four young women in the car. The two on the passenger side turned to face Will and yanked up their sweaters and bras exposing their breasts. They were really quite lovely too. Will laughed and gave them a thumbs-up as they sped off into the night.

About another ten miles or so up the highway, there was a restaurant/bar on the side of the road, Hernando's Hideaway, Steaks & Seafood. There were many cars parked in front, always a good sign, and one of them was the same car with the girls that had passed him just a few minutes earlier. Before he could even think about it, Will whipped into the parking lot and headed inside. It was crowded. Just about every table was taken. The girls with the pretty breasts were at a table with a batch of fellows drinking beer and eating peanuts. One of them noticed Will and gave him a big smile. He gave her another thumbs-up but decided to leave well enough alone.

There was an empty table toward the back near the door going into the kitchen and he went to it. Almost immediately, a young woman appeared at the table with menu and pad. "You are not from around here, and I am going to guess from the looks of you that you are not going to order Pabst or Black Label. Michelob is going to be about the best I can offer you."

"Michelob suits me fine," Will replied as he accepted the menu.

Within a few moments, she was back with two bottles of Michelob. She sat down. Handed one Michelob to Will and kept one for herself. "My name is Liza. It's been a long evening. If you don't mind putting up with my chatter, I'll rest my feet but will see that you get the best meal in the house promptly served." Without waiting for an answer, she handed the order slip to one of the other waitresses who disappeared into the kitchen with it.

In no time, steak, sautéed onions, mushrooms, a loaded bake potato and house salad arrived. All were excellent. Will ate heartily while Liza chattered on about football in general and the Sugar Bowl in particular.

Suddenly there was a loud crash from out front. Then another and another and another. One of the waitresses ran to Liza and said, "It's Donald!"

Liza jumped up, grabbed Will's arm and said, "Come on right now. That's your car being worked over with a baseball bat. I'm pretty sure you are to be next."

"How do you know it's my car?" Will asked.

"Look, if you want to go out there and check, be my guest. I don't recommend it," Liza said as she yanked Will through the kitchen door, through the kitchen and out into the back parking lot. They headed for what Will guessed was Liza's car parked to the far side of the lot, but then she abruptly stopped. A battered old pickup loaded with two 55-gallon drums of garbage was just starting to leave.

Liza waived it down and told the driver to ease on out like he always did and go on to the dump like always but not to stop for anyone no matter what. Will and Liza then climbed into the back of the pickup and lay down flat on the bed as the old truck rumbled out of the yard. The old truck headed down the highway for about 15 minutes and eventually turned off onto a dirt road. Then, a couple of miles or so down the dirt road, Liza banged on the cab of the truck to stop it and told the driver to go ahead and dump his garbage as usual and then go on home. If anyone asked, he had not seen her or anyone else and if he valued his balls, he would never tell anyone that he had given Liza a ride or where he had dropped her off.

As soon as he was out of sight, Liza turned and headed back up the road with Will in tow. About a hundred yards back was a farmhouse on one side of the road and a barn on the other. They headed for the barn. Once inside they eased down a long narrow corridor to a ladder, which they climbed up into the hayloft.

Liza then said, "We need to spend the night here. The Conners live in the house across the road. They both work. As soon as they leave for work in the morning, we can go in their house and use the phone. You are going to have to call someone to come pick you up."

"First," Will asked, "how do you know it was my car that whoever was beating up on? Second, how are we going to get in that house?"

"Come on. First of all, did your car have an Alabama tag on it? Every other car in the parking lot did. Wake up. Second, nobody around here ever locks their doors. Sooner or later, they are going to see that someone made a long distance call on their phone but they won't know that until their phone bill comes. That might be a week or a month but either way, you should be long gone."

Hay bales were stacked everywhere. It was cold but Will figured that they could stay reasonably warm buried in the hay particularly if they stayed together. They needed to make a nest among the bales so Will started shifting hay bales around and soon had a small tunnel. He took off his leather jacket and invited Ms. Liza into their newly assembled nest for the night. They crawled in together. She lay with her back up next to Will. He pulled his leather jacket up over their shoulders for warmth. He put one arm under her head. She snuggled up closer to him. He put his other arm around her waist and drew her a little closer still.

After a few minutes of silence, Will had to ask. "Who the hell is Donald? Is he your husband or something? What have I gotten into?"

Liza suddenly turned over so that they were face to face. "He's not my husband—that's for sure. Never has been and never will be. It's really kind of complicated though. I run Hernando's. My mother, sister and I own it. My father started it when he got back from World War II and it was very successful from day one. He

35

died a few years ago. I was in my third year at Auburn majoring in American history and education. I was going to be a high school English and American history teacher. When he died, I returned home immediately, of course, and then opened Hernando's back up immediately after his funeral. I really had no other choice. It is and always has been very profitable. It was putting me through college. My mother teaches high school English. She was not ready to retire and really did not have any interest in Hernando's anyway. My younger sister was still in high school. It was either me take it over, close it or sell it. I took it over.

"It has really worked out well. I had worked there all through high school. I had done it all—washed dishes, waited tables, cashiered, bought supplies. You name it. I did it. So much for becoming a high school history teacher. Actually, the irony is that I have been making more money running Hernando's than my mother makes teaching high school, and she has been teaching forever.

"At some point after I re-opened Hernando's, Donald and I started dating. You might say that we became an item. Then he went into the Army and ultimately got shipped off to Korea. We wrote for a while, but then his letters came further and further apart until they finally stopped altogether. At that point, I stopped writing too. About a month ago, he got out of the Army and came home. But he's changed. He is an entirely different person. He is short-tempered, impatient with everybody and everything. Sometimes he is just plain mean. I have refused to go out with him anymore or to have anything to do with him. But he always knows where to find me, Hernando's. I don't know what I am going to do. I don't even know if there is anything I can do. And I really believe he was going to hurt you and maybe me last night."

Will couldn't see Liza even though she was right in front of him. About then, one of them sort of shifted a little. Then the other tried to move a little closer. Will sought her with his lips and kissed her on the forehead. She turned her face up to him. He found her lips and kissed her softly, then brought his hand up to her cheek. Without saying a word, they kissed again and then again and again, again, again and again.

CHAPTER ELEVEN

At daybreak, they were awakened by car doors closing and an engine starting. As the car drove off, they dug themselves out of their hay cave, stood up and stretched. Will held Liza close for a moment, kissed her briefly, and then they headed down the ladder from the loft and across the road to the Conner's house. The Conner's car was gone and, as Liza had predicted, the house was unlocked.

Once inside, Will picked up the phone, dialed the Oxford, Georgia, Police Department, and got Ed Jenkins, Chief of Police, on the phone.

"Ed, I need a lot of big favors fast, no questions asked. My life may be on the line. Put R.T. and Kurt in one of your unmarked but obvious police cars and send them to pick us up in Alabama. I'm going to put Liza on the line in a minute and she will tell you exactly where we are. They need to be prepared for big trouble, but I really don't expect that it is going to come to that, though." Then he gave the phone to Liza.

Liza gave Ed precise directions to where they were, and then gave the phone back to Will.

"Ed, two more things. Tell them to fill up with gas just before they pick us up. Once we are in the car, there are not to be any stops until we are back into Georgia. Also, tell them to pull up in front of the barn, turn around on the road and wait. Don't honk. Don't get out. Just keep the engine running and wait. We'll pick the moment to get in the car just in case we sense complications."

Will hung up and turned to Liza. She had a funny look on her face. "You just told him that they are to pick us up. Am I going too?"

"Absolutely. You are in this mess because of me. There is no way I am going to let you go back and deal with that nutcase by yourself. Now, let's get back to the barn. It is going to be a cold several hours before they get here, and I don't think we ought to stay in this house a minute longer than we have to. We need to be in the barn and out of sight."

They headed back to their hay cave. Within minutes, they were snuggled up close together. Then a little closer. Then a soft kiss. "Thank you for wanting to protect me and for looking after me," Liza whispered. "That was very nice." Another soft kiss and then another and another and ultimately wonderful sleep....

Late afternoon, they heard a car drive slowly down the road, turn around and stop. Looking between the boards of the hayloft, they could see what was obviously an unmarked police car containing two uniformed officers. Will and Liza were down the ladder and across the yard in seconds. As they approached the car, the back door swung open. They literally dove in on the back seat and in an instant were heading back up the road.

After an hour or so on the road back toward Georgia, Liza and Will cautiously sat up, stretched a bit and began to relax. She reached over and held his hand. He eased over a little closer to her and put her hand in his lap. She put her head on his shoulder and was sound asleep in seconds.

As they pulled into Will's driveway, the tires crunching on the pea gravel woke Liza up. She sat up and looked around. "You live here? Who the hell are you?"

Even in the dark, it was an imposing place. "I'm not anybody. I actually live in a small carriage house behind this very nice main house. It is owned by Mrs. Calhoun. She is the widow of T. J. F. Calhoun, founder of Oxford First National Bank, and she lives alone in the main house. I don't pay much rent because I take care of the grounds for the entire estate."

R.T. and Kurt drove to the back of the property and stopped in front of the carriage house. Liza and Will went in, turned on heat and lights, and then held each other until the room warmed up a bit. Liza stared for a few minutes, and then said, "This place is a damn museum. Where did you get all of this stuff?"

"My parents were killed in a plane crash while I was in school. I was their only child so I inherited everything. My mother had inherited some family heirlooms and then collected antiques over the years. She was on a first name basis with every antique dealer in Atlanta. As a hobby, I make copies of Williamsburg furniture, which is mixed in with what I inherited from her. Now, what can I get you?"

"What I want most in the world right now is a long hot bath."

"There is a thick terry cloth robe folded up on the shelf in the closet in the bathroom along with towels, soap, and shampoo, everything I think you might need. Help yourself."

As Liza headed for the bathroom, Will lit the previously laid fire logs, propped his feet up on the coffee table in front of the sofa, and promptly fell sound asleep.

Much later, he awoke. The fire had burned down. There was a slight chill in the air. He looked for Liza. She was sound asleep in his bed buried under the comforter. He got a blanket and pillow out of the hall closet so as not to wake her, and then he stretched out on the sofa.

CHAPTER TWELVE

At 6:30 the next morning, Will woke up, a carryover from Citadel days. He went to the kitchen and started coffee, thawed and then started toasting a bagel. Good to be back home.

Coffee aroma began wafting through the house, and shortly Liza appeared wrapped in Will's bathrobe. She stood there quietly for a few minutes, then finally said, "I asked you once before, and now I ask you once again. Who the hell are you?"

"OK. OK. Don't jump to conclusions. I am really not anybody. My name is Will Hampton. We are in Oxford, Georgia, outside of Atlanta where I teach at a small, elite, two-year college that feeds students to Emory in Atlanta. As I explained last night, I rent this carriage house behind Mrs. Calhoun's main house. I really could not afford the rent on even this, except that I do the yard work and maintain the buildings, of which there are several."

"Ed Jenkins that I called to pick us up is the police chief in Oxford," Will continued. "He is a lot older than me but we are best friends. Now that I think about it, Ed is best friends with everybody that he knows which is everybody in Oxford and many outside Oxford." He further explained that he had been in New Orleans for the holidays and was on his way back home when he stopped at Hernando's.

"And now, dear Liza, what, might I ask, can I fix you for breakfast?"

Over coffee, Liza further explained how she and her sister now operated Hernando's. It was also obvious that dealing with the public had given her a sense of self-confidence that was both becoming and gracious.

As Will stood there and listened, he could only marvel. Here was the most straight forward and, at least to his eyes anyway, most attractive young women that he had ever met. Furthermore, she was a wonderful, enthusiastic, responsive lover.

He walked over to her. Put his arms around her and kissed her on the forehead. "My dear, you are absolutely lovely as you are but we need to make a trip downtown and get you some clothes and whatever else you might need. Then we need to go by my office and pick up my class rosters for the upcoming semester to see which classes made and when they meet."

"Professor, have you already forgotten? Your car was totally destroyed outside Hernando's night before last."

"Ah, that, dear lady, was a rental car. I have a little 1952 MG TD in the garage next door. It belonged to my dad. As I mentioned last night, my dad and mother were killed in a plane crash while I was in school. I always loved that little car so I did not sell it. I kept it for myself instead. Fortunately, I did not take it to New Orleans. It only seats a driver plus one passenger. Most of my friends live in or near the Quarter and don't even own cars. I needed a larger car that could transport the masses so I got a rental. We have transportation right here for us any time we need it. Now, it is going to be a little while before stores start opening downtown, my dear. Why don't we use that time to get better acquainted with each other?"

He reached over, gently pulled her to him by the collars of the bathrobe, and gently kissed her. Then he reached down, untied her robe, and reached inside.

CHAPTER THIRTEEN

Within a few days, it was obvious that Will did not want Liza to leave, ever. She was very bright, inquisitive and a marvelous lover. She did not appear to be in any rush to leave. In fact, she had called her sister to say that she was safe, happy and that she would not be home right away.

Then, a few days later, Will was grading papers in his office when he got a phone call from Mildred Johnson, a librarian at the Oxford Public Library.

"Dr. Hampton. There is a young woman here applying for a library card. She put your address down as her address. You live behind Mrs. Calhoun, don't you? This young lady doesn't have a driver's license or any kind of real ID. Is she OK?"

"Oh yes, Mrs. Johnson, she is quite OK and yes, we live in Mrs. Calhoun's Carriage House."

"Well, I didn't know you had gotten married, Dr. Hampton. Congratulations, young man. She is a very attractive young lady."

"Thank you. We really haven't announced anything yet. You are one of the first to know. We'll be going public very shortly, though."

"Well, since she belongs to you, I am going to issue Ms. Liza her library card without formal ID, etc. I am sure it will be all right."

"Yes, and thank you very much. By all means. Issue her a card and let her have whatever books she wants. By the way, since we haven't announced anything publicly, maybe you could keep it quiet for a bit."

"Oh yes, Dr. Hampton. You can count on me."

That evening, Will saw Liza's stack of library books on the sofa and glanced at the titles. They covered antique furniture, decorating, gourmet cooking and fashionable dress. Will thought to himself that it appeared that Liza was planning to stay a while.

CHAPTER FOURTEEN

N ext morning Will had hardly gotten situated in his office when there were the three quick signature raps of Dean J.O. Herring on his door and in came the Dean.

"Damn, son! I suggested you add a little frivolity into your life and you come back from Christmas break married. What the hell?"

"J. O., I went to New Orleans for the holidays. Had an absolutely wonderful time with old college friends. Ate wonderful food. Listened to jazz, blues, all kinds of great music..."

"Quit beating around the bush lad. You got married. I gotta have the details. Eleanor is all over me about this. It seems Mildred Johnson at the library scooped her on this one and Eleanor blames me for not knowing or worse, knowing and not telling her. You and your bride are invited for supper tonight at our place. It is a command performance. President Lester and his wife will be there and no telling who else. Now tell me about it so I can get back to running this college."

"Neither of us has enough time right now for me to even scratch the surface about the greatest thing that has ever happened to me.

Suffice it to say, I took your advice and was putting some frivolity in my life, but instead met Liza, the most wonderful creature on the planet. Now I have my morning chemistry class in five minutes, and you have a college to run. What time tonight?"

At noon, Will went home for lunch and broke the news to Liza that they had a command performance that night. When she opened the front door to let him in, she looked past him and gasped, "Donald!"

Walking down the driveway toward them was a young man with a .45 Army 1911 pistol in his hand. Will instinctively grabbed Liza and pushed her behind him and back through the front door.

Then one of the most amazing things Will had ever seen took place. Chief Jenkins came casually strolling down the driveway toward Donald. Donald spun around pointing the .45 at the Chief.

Chief Jenkins held out both of his hands showing that they were empty and very calmly said, "Just a minute Donald. I need your help. I am not going to arrest you. I'm not even carrying a gun. But I really do need your help."

"I've talked to your sheriff over in Alabama. He told me that you were in the Army and in Korea. He also told me that you are a good man and that you had an outstanding record in Korea. You see, I had a son. He was in the Army and he was also in Korea. He was killed there. He was the only child Frances and I had. We miss him terribly. I have many questions about Korea, about his unit, about where they fought, what it was like in Korea. There are a lot of things you could tell me. I mean you don't have to if you don't want to, of course. You are not under arrest or anything. You can leave anytime. Oh, by the way. Here are your car keys. I had it moved down to my office. Shouldn't leave keys in a car like that. Someone might steal it. Do you think you might spare an old man a little time to answer some of his questions? I certainly would be beholden to you."

Donald didn't say anything but kind of nodded.

Chief Jenkins continued. "Even though I am a police officer, I get a little nervous around guns. Would you mind terribly putting that pistol away at least while we talk? I don't mean for you to give it to me. I suspect you more than earned that pistol over in Korea. Just stick it in your belt or somewhere so that, if it goes off, it won't be my balls that get blown off.

"This isn't any kind of trick. As I said, you are not under arrest. You can leave any time you want too. Nobody is going to lay a finger on you unless, of course, you try to use that pistol."

At that point, Donald lowered the hammer on the .45, dropped out the magazine, cleared the round out of the chamber, and offered the pistol to Chief Jenkins.

Jenkins did not take it. "No, son. You keep it. Like I said, I bet you more than earned it in Korea. And also, like I said, you are not under arrest."

Jenkins paused for a second and continued. "Donald, we have the most wonderful bakery in the world just down the street from here. It's called Henri's. Henry Renoir— would you believe that he is a Frenchman?—escaped from France just as the Nazis took over. He moved here and opened his bakery. Been here ever since. I suspect he would have been killed had he stayed in France. But he is an amazing baker. He is down there every morning by 5:30, starting breads, rolls of all kinds, amazing stuff. Every day he makes what he calls his Roast Beef Po Boy sandwiches. Best anywhere. He starts with long loafs of French bread. He cuts them in half long ways, spreads Danish butter on both sides, then mayonnaise and some sort of special mustard. No lettuce. No tomato. Just roast beef, salami, ham, Swiss cheese and a thin kosher dill pickle slice. If we get a move on right now, he might still have one or two left."

Chief Jenkins and Donald strolled on down the driveway together and out of sight. R.T. and Kurt stepped out of the bushes with their rifles slung over their respective shoulders.

"No worry, folks." Kurt said to Will and Liza after they emerged from the house. "We had him in our sights every minute. But we were also betting that the Chief was going to win this one, too."

"Aren't you going to follow them?" Will asked.

Kurt looked over and said "Professor, Chief would have invited us if he had thought that he might need us. My bet is Donald will be out with the Chief on opening day of dove season and maybe even quail season. So long, sir."

Will turned around to Liza, but before he could say anything, she looked at him and said, "You would have made him shoot you before he could hurt me."

Will kissed her on the forehead and said, "I love you very, very much. Will you marry me?"

She buried her head in his shoulder, crying softly and said, "Oh God, yes. Yes, Yes, Yes."

They walked back into Carriage House together. "Liza, I have a confession to make."

"You are not going to tell me that there is already a Mrs. Hampton, are you?"

"Well, actually, yes. There is already a Mrs. Hampton. Do you remember yesterday when you got your library card? You know it says 'Liza Hampton' on it. When you did not have any ID and you gave this address as your address, which was fine, Mrs. Johnson, the librarian called me. She stepped into the back room under some pretense or the other and called me at the office to see if you were legit. I told her that you were indeed very legit and to issue you the card. She congratulated me on our marriage, and I told her we had not announced it publicly yet, but please issue you the card, which she did.

"You see, Georgia still has common law marriage. When you accepted that library card with your name on it as Liza Hampton, you acknowledged that we are married. You and I are husband and wife and have been since that moment. Your library card is our marriage certificate. Now that does not mean that we cannot have a ceremonial marriage. We can and should but right now we have a more immediate matter to deal with.

"We have been ordered to appear tonight at Dean Herring's for dinner so his wife, Eleanor, can meet you and can thereafter tell everyone that she has met you and approves of the match. President Lester and his wife will be there and no telling who else."

"You know of course, that I have absolutely nothing to wear to something like that," Liza said.

"There is a wonderful solution to that little problem. Call Eleanor Herring and explain that you do not have anything to wear tonight and ask her if she will take you on a quick shopping trip this afternoon so you can get something. It will make her day, and she will probably tell you that she doesn't have anything either and needs to get a little something. But enough for now. I have class. Take whatever money you need out of the cash in the top drawer of the desk and get whatever you need for tonight. I hate to leave, but I must. I have a lab full of Embryology students waiting on me."

CHAPTER FIFTEEN

That evening Will walked into the house after his last lab to change and get ready for the Herrings just as Liza walked out of the bedroom. She was absolutely beautiful with a much-understated elegance. Her light brown hair, which had heretofore just been pulled back, was now coiffed. She wore only the slightest touch of makeup along with a very soft touch of lipstick. She was simply the most beautiful creature Will had ever seen.

One more touch would fit perfect. Will went to his little fire-proof wall safe and removed a single strand of pearls that had belonged to his mother. He put them around Liza's neck. They were perfect for her. Then he thought of one more thing. He went back to the safe and removed a wide gold wedding band.

"Liza, I hope you will want this. It also belonged to my mother but it had been in our family from way back." He slipped it on her finger. It fit nicely. He gave her a soft lingering kiss. Finally, she pushed him away and said, "Later. Get in there and change clothes. We are going to be late to our own whatever if you don't get a move on."

Dr. Herring lived an easy walk from Mrs. Calhoun's. Will and Liza arrived just as the Lesters drove up. J.O. met them all at the door and promptly ushered them into a nicely appointed entrance hall where he took their coats and then invited them into the living room where there was a fire blazing in the fireplace. J.O. made a good living as Dean of the College but it was obvious from his and Eleanor's standard of living that there was additional income coming in from somewhere. Every visible room—the entrance hall, the living room and the dining room, which was across the entrance hall from the living room—tastefully displayed an amazing collection of southern antique furniture and fine art.

Liza leaned over and whispered to Will, "What is it with you people and old furniture. Won't you have anything less than 100 years old? I thought Carriage House looked like a museum. We've been out done, dear."

Eleanor magically appeared, introduced Liza to the Lesters, and passed hors d'oeuvres of chicken liver pate on toast points along with a wonderful pinot noir. J.O. then announced with great dignity, "This court of inquiry is now in session. Dr. Hampton, you have the burden of proof so you have to right to open and close. This court now rules on its own motion that you cannot waive opening statement. Please proceed, sir."

"Your Honor, Dr. Lester and ladies. While driving back from New Orleans the other night, I stopped at a restaurant/bar to perhaps say hello to two attractive young ladies who had just shown me their lovely breasts as we were driving down the highway. However, I was immediately most taken by this most lovely creature and was actually enjoying a very nice meal with her when we were forced to exit the restaurant through the kitchen and depart the premises concealed in the back of a garbage truck in order to escape certain death at the hands of a former 'acquaintance' of hers.

"We spent the night hidden in a hayloft until the next afternoon when our own Chief Ed Jenkins smuggled us back to Georgia. We have been together ever since and have been married only a few days. Liza has her library card to prove it. And with that, Your Honor, I rest my case."

"Will, my boy," J.O. said as laughter finally died down, "you spin a fine yarn. Now the truth please, sir."

"With all due respect, Your Honor, that is the truth. Now, the story of how Chief Jenkins dealt with my lovely wife's former acquaintance this afternoon will have to await another time."

"What! You say not only that all of this is true but that there is more. Good gracious, lad. How can this be?"

"How can it be? Very simple, I met the most wonderful creature on this planet, and I was not about to let her slip away."

"Liza. Would you like to add anything? Is he telling us the truth?"

"Well, all I can add is that he sure knows how to show a lady a good time on a first date. And he certainly makes a warm cozy nest in a hayloft on a cold winter night."

Mrs. Lester then spoke up to say, "Best story I have heard in I don't know when. Still not sure how much if any of it is true. But a marvelous story nevertheless."

At that point, Eleanor announced, "Junior has dinner ready. Let's not keep him waiting," and they all started across the entrance hall toward the dining room.

Will leaned over and whispered to Liza, "If Junior is William Mann, Jr., and I bet he is, then we are to witness life from a bygone era. William Mann, Jr., is a remnant from the time when wealthy families had live-in cooks. Some of those cooks were extraordinarily talented. William Mann, Jr., is generally acknowledged to be the best of the best. I thought he had retired, though."

Standing next to the door connecting the dining room with the kitchen was a short black man with gray hair wearing a starched white coat, black bowtie, starched white shirt, black pants and immaculately shined black shoes.

Eleanor went to Junior as they entered the dining room and said, "Junior, this is Dr. and Mrs. William Hampton. They have just been married a few days and tonight's diner is to welcome Mrs. Hampton into our college family. Thank you ever so much for doing your usual magic for us this evening. Liza, Junior is one of the greatest, if not the greatest, of the living southern cooks. He has cooked for my family whenever we needed him for years and he agreed to do the honors for us tonight even though he is largely retired."

They all sat and Junior began pouring wine at each place. Tomato aspic was passed around, followed by veal braised with white wine, wild rice and mushrooms, asparagus and stuffed Vidalia onions. Dessert followed—plum pudding with hard sauce— accompanied by tawny port. Will reached over and took Liza's hand under the table. He knew they were about to retire back to the living room for what would be delightful conversation, but he kept thinking that he would much rather hurry back to Carriage House and ravish his lovely bride.

They did retire back to the living room, followed by wonderful and entertaining conversation that is only exchanged between likeminded best friends. It had indeed been a wonderful Friday evening. By the end of the evening, they all realized that they had participated in one of those rare magical evenings created by new but rich friendships.

Liza and Will walked back to Carriage House. Will lit the previously laid fire in the living room fireplace, stood back up, took Liza in his arms and just held her close for a few minutes. He then whispered to her, "I am the luckiest guy on planet earth." He kissed her softly on her lips, then on her neck. He moved her over to the sofa where she unclasped her pearls and he began unbuttoning her blouse.

CHAPTER SIXTEEN

Early next morning, Will woke up at 6:30 as he always did. He moved over in search of Liza for a little conjugal activity after which he decided that, it being Saturday morning, it was a good morning to sleep in. Liza dozed off and on until about 8:00 when she then headed to the kitchen to start coffee.

There was a very attractive middle-aged black woman in the kitchen putting down her purse and taking off her coat.

Liza dashed back to the bedroom. "Will, Will wake up. There is a strange woman in the kitchen."

Will half way rolled over. "What does she look like? Is today Saturday? It's probably Rachel." And he rolled back over to sleep.

"Will, who is Rachel? What is she doing here?"

At last giving up and sitting up, Will explained, "If it is Saturday and she is black, middle age and attractive, she is Rachel and she is here to clean house and to do laundry."

"Then what am I to do?" Liza asked.

"Anything and everything she says to do. Nobody argues with Rachel and lives. Come on. Let me introduce you."

Will rolled out of bed, pulled on an old pair of Levis and a faded polo shirt and headed for the kitchen, coffee and Rachel but not necessarily in that order.

Rachel sort of came with the Carriage House. She actually worked Saturdays in the big house for Mrs. Calhoun but, on Mrs. Calhoun's instructions, always stopped off at Carriage House to keep it in good order. Mrs. Calhoun had said she could imagine what kind of housekeeper a young bachelor professor would be.

Once in the kitchen, Will introduced Liza as his wife before Rachel could make any comments about Will having sleep-over company again. Will then started coffee for everyone, broke out orange marmalade and English muffins before heading outside to start Mrs. Calhoun's yard work.

Once outside, Will noticed that Mrs. Calhoun's car was back in the garage, indicating that she was back in town. Will ambled over to the main house, climbed the back steps and knocked on the kitchen door.

Mrs. Calhoun opened the door, let him in and promptly told him, "I don't date married men. Just because I'm 71 years old and a widow doesn't mean that I'm a pushover."

"Mrs. Calhoun, you played too hard to get too long. I just could not wait any longer. People were going to start thinking that I wasn't interested in women or something. Why you weren't even in town over the holidays. We could have been off somewhere, having a grand old time spending some of your late husband's money."

"I finally figured out that I am just not the kind of woman that really appeals to you. I talked to Eleanor and she told me that you met your bride in a bar and then spent the night with her in a hayloft. I am just not that kind of woman. Now, truth be told, Eleanor did say that your wife is absolutely wonderful. Eleanor still doesn't quite understand how you convinced that wonderful young lady to marry the likes of you. Now, when am I going to meet her?"

"Any time you want to. She is very close at hand, you know. Right now she is getting acquainted with Rachel."

"Both of you come for lunch today, say about 12:30. Dress comfortable but no blue jeans."

"May we use the front door?"

"By all means. Back door is only for hired help. Now get out of here and go get some yard work done. And go out the way you came in, through the back door."

With that, Will headed out the back door to go tell Liza that they had another command performance at 12:30 that day.

Lunch was exquisite. Even though it was Saturday, Mrs. Calhoun had brought in her former cook, Daisy Redman, out of retirement for the occasion. Daisy's chicken salad was legendary. It was made with both pecans and fried bacon plus unknown spices. Daisy also prepared another of her creations, spinach soufflé with tomato sauce, and then old fashion whiskey cake for dessert.

As they finished lunch, Mrs. Calhoun took charge and said, "Liza, that common law marriage business may satisfy the laws of the State of Georgia, but it doesn't meet the standards of polite society in Oxford. We need to arrange a proper wedding for you and right away. Now, who in your family needs to be here and when can they get here?"

Liza's only family was her sister and mother, both of whom could be here any time.

"What we ought to do, then, is have a small private ceremony next Saturday, right here in the parlor, family only, and followed by a reception also here in the house. We will invite everybody we need to invite. You prepare your guest list and I'll add mine to it."

"Yes, ma'am," Liza answered.

"Liza, what church were you raised in? You were raised in a church, weren't you?"

"Oh, yes," Liza replied. "We are Methodist."

"Very good. I have already spoken to Reverend Smallwood, head pastor at Oxford First Methodist, and he is available Saturday afternoon. Eleanor is going to take care of food and beverage for the reception, and I'll handle the rest.

"Also," Mrs. Calhoun continued, "I have the Oxford Women's Club coming here tomorrow afternoon. They can address envelopes for the invitations. J.P. Stevens Co. will have the invitations ready for mailing late Monday afternoon. You two need to get me mailing lists by first thing tomorrow morning. What have I forgotten? Yes, one more thing. Liza, your mother and sister can stay here in the main house as my guests. I have nothing but room here. Now. What have I forgotten?"

A bewildered Liza looked at an even more bewildered Will and both could only say "Nothing."

As soon as they got back to Carriage House, Liza called her mother and sister. They were excited, delighted and immediately went into high gear. Liza had no more than hung up from talking to them but Eleanor called to say that she would be by to pick up Liza in 30 minutes so they could start looking for something for her to wear.

Liza turned to Will and asked, "Does anyone ever tell her no?"

All Will could say was, "Not that I'm aware of."

"Well, anyway, no more yard work for you today. We have lists to prepare."

CHAPTER SEVENTEEN

By Saturday night, the enormity of it all began to sink in, and Liza and Will really began thinking about the wedding and the upcoming week.

"My sister can stand up with me. Who are you going to have with you?" Liza asked Will.

"Walter Kelly, my roommate from The Citadel is my first choice. He is also close by. He teaches over at Georgia Tech now. What do you think?"

"Perfect," Liza replied.

By supper that evening both Liza and Will had completed their guest lists and delivered them to Mrs. Calhoun. They invited her to join them for supper, but she declined saying, "I'm way too busy. I have a wedding next Saturday to arrange."

Sunday morning Liza and Will joined Mrs. Calhoun at Oxford First Methodist for church and to meet the Rev. Smallwood. While they were chatting with Rev. Smallwood on the front steps after the service, he turned to Will and told him, "Will, your marriage shifts a lot of pressure on to me. Heretofore, you were the most eligible bachelor in town, and I could stay below the radar. Now, with you out of the picture, I am front and center by default."

Will replied, "Just leave everything to J. P. Stevens & Company. They will have you walking down the aisle before you even know it."

By Monday evening, it was all but a done deal. J. P. Stevens & Company had the envelopes to Mrs. Calhoun in time for her woman's club to address them Sunday afternoon, and delivered the actual engraved invitations first thing Monday morning. By Monday afternoon, they were delivered to the Post Office so that most would be delivered the next day. Eleanor Herring, on the other hand, had arranged a shopping trip for Wednesday with Liza, Liza's sister and mother to select Liza's wedding dress and dresses for the upcoming parties. Liza's mother and sister were scheduled to arrive Tuesday.

Wednesday afternoon there would be a tea at Eleanor Herring's for Liza, her mother and sister to meet the ladies of Oxford. Thursday the faculty wives were having a luncheon, and then Thursday evening there was a cocktail party at the Lesters' house. Friday evening was a short rehearsal in Mrs. Calhoun's parlor followed by a rehearsal dinner at Oxford Club.

Everything came off as J. P. Stevens & Company had decreed. Mrs. Calhoun's reception after the private ceremony turned out to be the high point of Oxford's social calendar for the year. Everyone was there. Everyone was relaxed and the mood was festive. Everyone loved Liza. She may have been from a small town in Alabama, but she had been, as the expression goes, "raised right."

Sarah Brinkman, secretary to Walter Kelly at Georgia Tech, was invited and came to the reception as, of course, did Walter. Sarah started giving Will a hard time that he owed her dinner, and then he ups and goes and gets married.

Sarah was a very attractive and bright young lady. Without saying a word, Will took her by the elbow and steered her across the room to where the Rev. James Smallwood was standing.

"James, I want you to meet Miss Sarah Brinkman. As you can see, she is very beautiful and, at least equally important, she is very bright. She is an Edna Calhoun or Eleanor Herring dynamo in the making. Sarah, this is the Rev. James Smallwood. Now, by his own admission, he is the most eligible bachelor in Oxford. And let me add, if his conduct at last night's rehearsal dinner is any indication, he is not an old stuff shirt either. You two should have a lot to talk about, and I need to go say hello to Chief Ed Jenkins."

Will and Liza along with Liza's mother and sister attended Oxford Methodist the next morning. They had no more than been seated when Sarah Brinkman slipped into the pew and joined them.

As has been a longstanding custom, Rev. Smallwood was standing on the front steps of the church greeting attendees as they filed out at conclusion of the service. Both Will and Liza noticed that, when Sarah and Smallwood shook hands, they held the clasp for what seemed like a bit longer than was usual under the circumstances. Will and Liza gave each other knowing glances. It seemed to them that Smallwood's reign as most eligible Oxford bachelor might well be ending sooner rather than later.

CHAPTER EIGHTEEN

M onday morning, Will was enjoying the hour or so break after his 9:00 class and before his 11:00 lab. Feet were up on
the desk. He was still savoring the memories of the last ten days,
Junior Mann's dinner at the Herrings, and the memory of the
love making that followed once he and Liza returned to Carriage
House. Then the parties in anticipation of the wedding and the
love making that followed each and every one. Of course the wedding, and of course the reception immediately afterward, and of
course the love making that followed. Ah, yes. Life is good. Then
came knocks on his door.

"Who goes there? Enter by all means."

Thomas R. Wheeler, IV, a student from last semester's
Comparative Anatomy class, stepped through the door, paused,
and looked around totally amazed.

Will's office was not what most expected by way of a college
professor's office. There were no diplomas, certificates, awards
or the like hanging on the walls. Instead, the office looked more
like a miniature Zoology museum. Hanging on the walls were

drawings of invertebrates that had been viewed through a micro-scope, anatomical drawings of dissected vertebrates and a pic-ture frame containing Will's insect collection prepared for Insect Study Merit Badge. Also hanging on the wall was an antique etching of the famous English surgeon/anatomist John Hunter, who was generally acknowledged the founder of comparative anatomy and scientific surgery. On top of one bookcase was the mounted skull of a saber-toothed tiger and what appeared to be the skull of an alien. The latter was actually a resin mockup Will had bought through Ward Scientific Supply simply because he thought it was really neat. He always told his students that he didn't know much about its origin. Only that it had come out of a crater near Roswell, New Mexico.

On Will's desk was a paperweight that was actually a fossilized Megalodon Shark's tooth about six inches long. Will had found it while he and Milby Burton, Director of the Charleston Museum, were sifting through tailings from the bottom of an old canal out-side of Charleston.

Also situated on Will's desk was a large specimen jar contain-ing a dissected shark's head exposing the cranial nerves. Will's re-discovery of the thirteenth cranial nerve in the shark had been the subject of Will's first published scientific paper written when he was still a junior at The Citadel. The thirteenth cranial nerve had been correctly identified more than 80 years earlier by a German anatomist but apparently forgotten or overlooked because all shark dissection manuals and thousands of comparative anatomy students had missed it over the years until Will came along and rediscovered it. Ironically, neither he nor his mentor, Col. I.S.H. Metcalf, could ever come up with any notion as to what that 13th cranial nerve's function might be. It was found to be present in humans in the early 1900s but its function in humans remained a mystery even fifty years later.

"Mr. Wheeler. Why aren't you in my Embryology class this se-mester? You were in Comparative Anatomy last semester. Have you abandoned study of the biological sciences? Have you ceased to be a disciple of John Hunter, Darwin and the great and wonderful Prof. William Hampton? What's to become of you?"

"Oh no, sir. I want to take Embryology. That is one of the things that I am here to talk to you about. I'm registering late. Dean Herring said I could still get in your Embryology class but only with your permission. May I?"

"By all means, Thomas. You did excellent work last semester in Comparative Anatomy. Where do I sign?"

"Right here, sir," Thomas said as he produced one of the college's late registration forms.

"You said that was one of the things you wanted to talk to me about. Is there something else I can do for you?

"Yes sir. Dr. Hampton, I have a pet lab, Ralph. Every now and then, we go out to one of the abandoned farms outside of town so he can romp around. We were out on Perkins Road late yesterday evening. There is a small abandoned farm on the south side of Perkins. The house, shack actually, fell in long time ago. Land itself hasn't been farmed, it seems, in years and years. Anyway, Ralph took off into the edge of the woods and then within a minute or so came running back with what I first thought was a stick. But it wasn't. It's part of a human humerus."

"Damn, lad. Are you sure?"

"Absolutely, sir. Last semester in Comparative Anatomy you made us identify the human bones blindfolded. It's the proximal end of the humerus. Humerus isn't even one of the tough ones to identify. I can even tell you that it is the left humerus."

"Where is the bone now?"

"Right here, sir." And Thomas handed over a small brown paper bag. "I really was not quite sure what to do with it. As you can see, it's been outside a long time."

"Thomas, you get an A+ on bone identification today. Definitely the proximal end of a human left humerus. Any idea whose farm it is or was?"

"I don't even know if it has an owner. It's one of those small family farms that has been abandoned for years."

"Every piece of land has an owner even if they are not obviously present. Years ago, people used to bury their dead family members in small family plots located somewhere on their property. No doubt, some graves were dug deeper than others were. Erosion over the years may have uncovered all or part of somebody's grave. This bone is definitely old enough to have been from that time."

Will stood and said, "I'm going over to the Tax Assessor's office at the Courthouse to find out who owns the property. Then I'm going to make a quick run out there and see if I can find any more of old Yorick lying around. Care to join me?"

"I'd really like to, sir. Kind of like solving a mystery, but I have to complete registration today or else."

CHAPTER NINETEEN

In the bowels of the Courthouse, Will was quietly sifting through the Tax Assessor's records searching for a farm on the south side of Perkins Road with a fallen in house or shack. He had just found a twenty-five acre farm that had to be the property when a loud boisterous voice called out his name, brought all activity in the entire building to an immediate halt, and turned every head in Will's direction.

"Professor, are you invading my domain and undertaking the practice of law now?"

"I wouldn't think of it, James."

James McAllister had recently left a very promising career with a large and very prestigious downtown Atlanta law firm and moved to Oxford to become a country lawyer.

"One of my students found part of a human skeleton out on an old farm on Perkins Road while walking his dog last night. I'm tracking down the owner of the property to see if I can go on the property and perhaps locate the rest of the skeleton."

"Well, Professor, looks like you have found it. It's owned by Oxford Farmers and Merchants Bank according to the Tax Assessor's report. Looks like Oxford Farmers and Merchants Bank acquired it through foreclosure in December 1950 by virtue of a mortgage from C. Williams, a man of color. C. Williams received the property by deed of gift from his father, Alpha Williams, in 1915. Alpha acquired the property by deed of gift from his former master, Thomas R.R. Holloway, dated September 1866. There you have it, Professor. No charge either," and with that James ambled on out.

Reading the Tax Assessor's notes further, Will noted that C. Williams borrowed $450.00 from Oxford Farmers and Merchants Bank in 1946 and put up the homestead as security for the loan. Apparently, he defaulted at some point and the bank foreclosed.

Will picked up his notes and headed down the street to Farmers and Merchants Bank. Calvin Perdue, current President and owner of the bank, was old enough to have been around when C. Williams borrowed from the bank in 1946.

CHAPTER TWENTY

Once inside the bank, Will was promptly shown into Mr. Perdue's desk at the back of the banking floor. After pleasantries, Will stated that he was interested in the property owned by the bank out on Perkins Road.

"Professor, we will not only be glad to sell you that property. We will all but pay you to take it off our hands. We might even do that. We have owned that property for years. Really sad situation. Had to foreclose on the black family that owned it. Mr. whatever-his-name-was was injured in World War I. He scratched out a small living on the place but got to the point that, physically, he could no longer do much work. About that time, his son came home from World War II. He helped for a while. Worked maintenance for the city and worked the farm. He was kind of full of himself, though. Guess he finally got tired of small town life and moved away. It was downhill for the old man after that.

"There's twenty-five acres, more or less, out there. Both of the buildings fell in long time ago. Professor, if you are looking to become a gentlemen farmer, this is just the place to start."

"Mr. Perdue, I have a piece of a human skeleton that was found on the property yesterday. I was wondering if perhaps there were some family graves somewhere on the property, and one might have gotten partially opened by animals or erosion. Do you know if there is a family plot somewhere out there anywhere?"

"I have no idea," Perdue replied. "I have been by the property but never on the property. We made that loan based on strength of character not collateral. Those folks were good folks. They were respectful and knew their place. They acquired that property as a gift after getting their freedom. My father knew that family well. We started this bank back before The Civil War. We really did not want to foreclose on them. In fact, we held off for several years in hopes the son would make a go of it. Maybe something good would turn up for those folks. Didn't think we would still own the property this many years later. Are you sure you don't want to become a member of the landed gentry?"

Will got up, "Thank you, but no thank you, Mr. Perdue. I have taken up way too much of your time. Thank you very much for the offer, though. You have been most helpful. Do you mind if I drive out there and look around?"

"Not a bit, Professor, and remember, it can be had for almost nothing. For you, we will even finance the entire purchase price."

"Once again, thank you very much, Mr. Perdue."

CHAPTER TWENTY-ONE

Will left the bank and went to Carriage House. "Liza, want to go for a stroll in the woods looking for old bones?" As expected, she was game even though it was still cold outside.

They both put on warm old clothes and headed out of town for Perkins Road. Locating the property was no problem. All other property on both sides of Perkins Road was under cultivation. About half of the bank's twenty-five acres had once been farmed, and the other half was old-growth hardwood forest. They left their car in what had once been the front yard and headed for the tree line along the same path Thomas Wheeler and his dog Ralph had created through the dead sagebrush.

Upon entering the woods, Will suggested that they spread out fifteen feet or so in order to cover more land. As they were walking along the bottom of a hill, Will was somewhat ahead of Liza. Looking at the ground in front as he walked, he saw what was obviously a piece of an Indian arrowhead. He reached down to pick it up just as a rifle shot rang out and the bullet hit the tree next to where Will's head had been.

He dropped completely to the ground, lying next to a rock about a foot high. He motioned to Liza to stay back and then said in a stage whisper, "I'm going to make a dash for that large tree just ahead of me. The minute I start, you run for the car as fast as you can and go get help. Don't stop even if you hear more shots. I'll be fine. Trust me. Now get ready."

In an instant he was up and sprinting to the large oak tree about ten feet ahead. At the same instant, another rifle shot rang out and went through the brush right behind him. And at that same instant, Liza was off and running back toward their car.

"Time," he thought. "I've got to stall for time. I've got to keep moving. I've gotta keep moving until Liza can get back here with the cavalry. But how? Gotta keep moving so he can't improve his position or close on me."

"He is somewhere up on that hillside. Downhill shots can be tricky. Maybe I can throw him off if I move closer and then further away each time I move."

Will dashed away from the hillside to a large tree behind and somewhat to the right of the large tree where he had been standing. Immediately, another shot rang out but it was way high. Without waiting another second, Will sprinted toward the hillside and to the left about twenty-five feet. He was already behind his next tree before the next shot rang out. He quickly took three steps back toward his last tree, then reversed direction and headed away from the hillside to another tree. Two more shots rang out, but both were way short. He looked around to plan his next move. About ten yards further into the woods was a deep creek bed. He ran zigzag toward the creek and slid feet first into the gully formed by the creek. Other shots rang out, but again they were nowhere close.

Will leaned hard against the inside of the gully and tried to catch his breath all the while thinking, "Damn good thing that it's a crisp winter day and there are no snakes moving around out here."

Another shot rang out but the bullet went into the far side of the gully over ten yards away. "Damn! Is that son of a bitch ever going to run out of ammo? At least he doesn't know where I am in the creek bed. Which way to go in the gully—back toward the car or away from the car? Away. He will expect me to go back."

Will started crawling on all fours up the gully away from the home place. He stopped every few seconds to listen if the shooter was moving around. "Was he coming down the hill, closing in?" he wondered.

Then way off in the distance there was the faint wail of a siren. "Yes, god damn it, yes. Only got to hold out a few more minutes. Surely, he will haul ass as soon as he hears the siren. My damn luck, he's deaf as well as a piss poor shot."

The siren was getting close. Real close. There was more than one. Maybe more than two.

"By god, bring it on."

Will cautiously peeked up over the top of the edge of the gully. Three more shots rang out in quick succession, but all three were aimed down the gully away from where he was hunkered down in the creek bed.

He stayed where he was in the gully until he heard Chief Jenkins calling his name. He answered back that the shooter had been up on the hillside and might still be there.

Kurt and R.T., both from Jenkins's office, and two deputies from the sheriff's office—all armed with shot guns—spread out and headed up the hill moving from tree to tree, first one then another.

Will then climbed out of the gully and headed to the Chief. Together they started walking back toward the homestead. As they broke through the tree line, Liza dashed forward and hugged Will.

He kissed her on the forehead. "Thank you. Thank you, darling. Let's go home."

Will turned back to Chief Jenkins. "Ed, somewhere out there, there is a human skeleton that someone does not want found. Here is the top part of his left arm. It's probably fairly close to the tree line. One of my students had his dog out here yesterday evening. The dog went into the woods and came out moments later with this bone fragment. Until the shooting started, I thought that the fragment probably came from an old family grave that had eroded open."

Will and Liza turned to leave but Jenkins stopped them, saying, "Will, you need to keep this with you for a while," and handed him a snub nose .38 Special. "Also, drive my police car over there for a few days. That little MG of yours is probably the only one in Georgia outside of Atlanta. Besides, I have wanted to take yours for a spin for quite a while anyway."

Will and Liza got into the police car. "Thank you again. Thank you very much. Now let's get out of here."

They pulled into the garage that abutted Carriage House and entered the house through the door that connected the garage with the house. As they entered the house, the phone started ringing. They looked at each other. "Do we answer it?" Liza ask.

"Why not? Can't get shot through the phone," Will said as he picked up the phone.

"Will, Ed Jenkins here. We have a pretty complete skeleton partially buried in a grave next to several other graves. Shoulder is all that is exposed. Your bone fragment appears to be the only missing part of the exposed skeleton. Rock slabs mark each of the graves but there are no names visible on any of them. Looks pretty much like you originally thought. It's an old family plot with a grave eroded partially open.

"Also, as you no doubt expected, our shooter was gone by the time the boys got to the top of the hill. They tracked him on out to the road and found where he had parked his car. They picked up a lot of brass from where he was shooting on the hillside. He threw a lot of lead at you, my boy."

"Damn right he did. I didn't think that he was ever going to run out of ammo. Seemed to me that he must have brought an entire case with him."

"Will, as you have no doubt realized, we have a hell of a mystery on our hands. There is obviously something out there somewhere that someone does not want to be found. I don't know if it is somehow tied into the skeleton with the bone fragment you had or if it is totally unrelated to your skeleton. I posted a deputy hidden out there to see if anyone returns and if they do to see what they go looking for."

Jenkins continued, "Now, real reason I called was to tell you that Kurt or R.T. or one of the sheriff's deputies will be guarding your house tonight and staying with you until we can sort this out. Whoever was shooting at you doesn't know what you found or did not find. We think you are pretty safe at school but they will stay with you even there as well. You get a good night's sleep tonight, but we need to talk first thing tomorrow. Now, what's your schedule like tomorrow? Be thinking back on who knew about the bone and that you were going out to that property."

"I'm out of class about 10:00 AM tomorrow and then don't have anything until lab at 1:30 PM," Will replied.

"I'll be at your office on campus at 10 in the morning and will bring our lunch with me. I don't want you moving around outside any more than absolutely necessary. I'm also alerting campus police to stop anybody on campus that does not have student ID or is not faculty, even if it's the governor. Lock your doors tonight if you haven't already. Don't answer any knocks unless one of our men says it's OK first. Draw all of your curtains and pull your shades down. Do I need to send you and Liza over some supper?"

"Thanks, Ed. We are in great shape here. We have plenty of leftovers from Saturday's reception. We should be inviting you and Frances for supper. Thank you, though. And thank you for thinking of everything."

Will hung up and turned to Liza. "Thank you again. Don't know how much longer I could have kept him faked out, whoever the hell he is." Then he plopped down on the sofa, pulling Liza down with him. "How about dessert before supper tonight?"

CHAPTER TWENTY-TWO

R.T. drove Will to class early next morning. Already the campus was abuzz. Anyone who had not heard about the shooting quickly figured out something was afoot. R.T. was at Will's side every minute. His police car was parked in Will's regular parking place. Dean Herring met them as they entered Science Hall.

"Will," R.T. said, "we have pulled down all of the shades of every window in the building. Don't want any windows shot out around here. It would cause too much paper work. Will, we have also switched you over to the classroom across the hall from your regular room. Campus police are stationed at every entrance to Science Hall and will be until this is over. Furthermore, only students, faculty and staff with picture IDs can even get on this part of campus. Hell, even the governor won't be able to get in until this is over."

Will had first thought that he might as well have cancelled class for the day. Most of his students might not want to be around him under the circumstance. But he did not want to appear to be a coward, and he knew he was going to have to face the student's questions sooner or later. Might as well get started.

Their reactions were not anything at all as Will had thought they might be. Class attendance was 100%. Not only that, they were ready to protect him from the rest of the world. They were ready to take on the shooter plus anybody and everybody else. They really wanted to duke it out with the shooter. They were ready to go to Perkins Road and search every inch of the property. They wanted to see the bone, which of course Will no longer had. Thomas Wheeler, IV, was fielding almost as many questions as Will. He was man of the hour. He had actually made a connection between what they had studied in class last semester and the real world. Very little class time was devoted to Embryology that day.

Chief Jenkins was waiting in Will's office along with Sheriff Cobb when class was over. They were carrying several sacks containing their three lunches, and Will got Cokes from his refrigerator in the lab.

It seemed that Perkins Road was actually outside Oxford's city limits, hence outside Jenkin's jurisdiction. Jenkins and Cobb were best of friends, though. There was no issue of competition or rivalry between departments. In fact, Cobb had deputized Jenkins so he could lawfully act in the county if need be.

First question was, of course, who knew Will was going to be out on Perkins Road? Will didn't have to think long to answer that question.

"To begin with," Will stated, "everyone in the courthouse knew I was going to Perkins Road and why. When I was researching ownership of the property, everybody in there heard me tell James McAllister about the bone and why I was checking ownership of the property. Then, everyone in the bank after I talked to Perdue, including of course, Perdue himself, knew about the bone. By the time Liza and I actually got out to the property, everybody in Oxford probably knew."

Second question was obviously, "What was out there worth shooting someone over?" Shooting seemed counterproductive. It only drew attention to the area. Sheriff Cobb pointed out that it was still not unusual for an old timer to make a little whiskey on a creek in an isolated area where he would not be readily detected. And it would not be at all unusual for that moonshiner to take a shot at any stranger approaching his still. Cobb further pointed out that if that were the case, Will would be safe as long as he stayed off Perkins Road.

"We might have an answer pretty soon if that is what is going on out there. Our moonshiner will try to recover his still before it can be found and cut down. Copper stills represent a substantial investment both in time and skill required to build plus cost of materials. That amount of copper doesn't come cheap." Cobb laughed and went on, "You know they used to teach industrial arts here in high school. Well, we got a new industrial arts teacher in one year. He could not understand why most of his students could solder a perfect straight seam every time. Someone had to finally clue him in that those boys were brought up soldering still seams."

Will laughed out loud and pointed out he had been unable to understand why some of his freshman chemistry students had been so knowledgeable about distillation apparatus and procedure when the lab assignment had been to separate benzene from ethanol by distillation.

Moving on, all agreed that Cobb's men would continue watching the property in hopes that the shooter would return and thus provide some answers. If no one showed up within a day or so, then old-fashioned police work dictated that the property had to be walked and searched for something worth shooting someone over. In the meantime, Jenkins's men would continue guarding Will.

CHAPTER TWENTY-THREE

Two days later Kurt leaned into Will's office to tell him that a still had been found on the creek downstream from where Will had hidden from the shooter. "Professor, have you ever seen a whiskey still? You being a chemistry and biology professor, thought you might find it interesting."

Kurt and Will went by Carriage House and picked up Liza. She was entitled to see what had caused all the ruckus. They drove to Perkins Road, and the three of them entered the wooded part of the property just as Liza and Will had done before. It was more than just a bit unnerving, for Will especially. He kept looking up the hill expecting to see someone. He passed the tree where the first shot would have hit him in the head had he not bent over to pick up the arrowhead. This time he picked up the arrowhead and without incident. They followed the creek downstream until they found where Sheriff Cobb, Ed Jenkins and several deputies were standing around what was obviously a still. They were taking turns having their pictures taken in front of it. Will had to admire the craftsmanship that had gone into designing and constructing the still. It was just perfect.

Liza looked closely at the still and remarked "Yep, just like my uncle used to make."

Will stood by as Jenkins and Cobb discussed age and estimated output. It was not operating now but had been very recently. Cases of Mason jars were stacked over to one side. There was a well-worn path alongside the creek, which evidently led to another road and access point.

Liza had wandered over to a large nearby rock and sat down waiting for the boys to get tired of being boys. They were looking at the still and having their pictures taken beside it. After Will had finally seen and heard enough, he joined Liza on the rock. Though he was thoroughly fascinated by the still, it appeared that the mystery was now solved, and he was ready to head home and resume a normal life.

As Will and Liza started to walk back upstream she asked, "What are those depressions in the ground over there?"

Will looked over to where Liza was pointing. There were two areas about six feet apart where the soil was sunken down eight inches or so. They looked like they had once been short trenches. Each was about two feet wide and five feet or so long.

Will turned back to the still. "Ed, Sheriff Cobb, you need to come over here. Take a look."

Cobb and Jenkins turned and looked to where Will was pointing. Cobb turned back to Jenkins and said "Oh shit. Ed, you thinking what I'm thinking?"

Jenkins replied, "I don't think those depressions have anything to do with the whiskey business, do you?"

Cobb turned to Kurt. "Kurt, why don't you take the Hamptons back home and, if you don't mind, when you get back up to your car, radio my office and tell my dispatcher to have all available deputies get out here with shovels. And tell my dispatcher to call the State Crime Lab in Atlanta. Have her tell those boys to start packing up their stuff and heading this way."

"Ed, this doesn't look good. Not a damn bit good. One such depression could be anything. Two like that though. It doesn't look good at all. I guess we ought to spread out and see if there are others while we are waiting on shovels."

Liza and Will headed back up the creek hand in hand. Neither could say a word.

Later that evening, Liza and Will were sitting together on their sofa in front of the fireplace after a rather somber supper when the phone rang. They knew it had to be Ed Jenkins or Sheriff Cobb.

It was Cobb. "Will, can you come over to the funeral home? We found three graves— including the two by the still—before it got too dark to keep looking. We opened up all three and brought the bodies over here to the funeral home. It will be at least tomorrow before anyone from the State Crime Lab can get here and, even then, their pathologist probably won't be with them. It seems that he is tied up testifying in some case down in Waycross, Georgia. Anyway, Ed and I thought that you might be able to tell us a little about what we have and kind of give us a head start. Kurt or R.T., whoever is guarding you, can bring you over."

While at The Citadel, Will's faculty advisor and mentor, Col. Doyle, had taught gross anatomy part time down the street at The Medical College of South Carolina. Will often accompanied him and participated in those labs.

During summer vacations, Will had worked in the operating rooms of one of the Atlanta hospitals. While there, he had become acquainted with and was befriended by Dr. John T. Godwin, the hospital's pathologist. Godwin was a giant in the Atlanta medical community and was often consulted by Georgia's State Crime Lab. On many of those occasions, he brought Will along, as he said, "for company who could talk."

Upon entering the workroom in the funeral home, Will immediately saw three bodies on adjacent worktables. It was immediately obvious that all three were young women and that all three had been buried nude. Their varying degrees of decomposition showed that they had been buried at varying times, probably over ten to fifteen years though the most recent had only been in the ground for a year or so. Two of the corpses were Caucasian. One, the most recently buried, was Negro.

Will first asked, "How deep were they buried?"

Cobb replied, "All three were about two to three feet deep."

Will then said to no one in particular, "You know we are obviously dealing with a serial killer. We have three homicide victims apparently murdered by the same killer. It is kind of odd, though, that all three were buried that deep. Most murderers are lazy. They only bury their victims a foot or so deep. Some only cover their victims with leaves or brush. That suggests that the killer cared enough about his victims that he wanted them to have decent burials. Or, he was trying to be sure that the remains would not be readily discovered by anyone or by wild animals. It probably means that he was making extra effort so that the bodies would not be found."

Will continued, "In any event, two are especially well preserved. That is due, in part, to the depth at which they were buried but more so to the nature of the soil that they were buried in. They were buried in moist, boggy soil at the bottom of a hill and next to a creek. Wet boggy soil slows decomposition. You have no doubt read about bodies preserved thousands of years in peat bogs. The third body appears to have been buried the longest. She also appears to be the most decomposed. She had to have been buried in dry clay up the hillside.

"It also appears that all three young women were pregnant when they were murdered. Most of their digestive tracts have decomposed. That has left the very visible "bump" in the pelvic region, which is almost certainly their respective uteri. All three uteri are too large not to contain a fetus. We could determine that for sure by examining the uteri but we should not disturb their bodies by making any kind of incisions. That must be left for the pathologist.

"We will also leave determination of cause of death for the pathologist. All three were probably strangled, though. See the bruising around their necks. That occurred in the moments before death and was caused by their strangulation. Again, we can't make any incisions, but I bet, if we opened the throat, we would find that the hyoid bone at the larynx of each victim is broken or crushed. It is the only bone in the body that is not connected to another bone. Strangulation almost invariably crushes it or at least damages it. That pretty well confirms strangulation as the cause of death. A cursory glance at their teeth shows professional dental care so all three were raised in families of some means.

"As for age, without looking at any of their bones, I'm going to guess late teens to mid-twenties. Hope that gets you at least started until you get the pathologist's report. He will be able to tell you a lot more, including age, by examining the ends of their bones where growth takes place."

Jenkins turned to Cobb and said what all three had been thinking. "Cobb, there is a serial killer killing young women from somewhere else and burying them in the Perkins Road woods. No young women have been reported missing from around Oxford in forever. We have no clue who they are or where they even came from. We can determine their respective heights. We know hair color and know that all are white except the most recent. She is Negro. This is not a rape murder scenario. All three were pregnant when murdered. They were almost certainly pregnant by their murderer. Therefore, there had to have been a consensual relationship of some sort up until and through early pregnancy. And we know that this sort of relationship had been going on for a number of years.

They probably came from Atlanta. Three missing young women from any town outside Atlanta would have attracted a lot of attention even if they had gone missing over a period of years. Atlanta is a melting pot for young people. If they were runaways or something, no telling where they came from. OK, now what have I left out and where does this leave us?"

All three stood there looking at each other. Finally Will said, "Well, we know at least three other things. First, our shooter probably lives right here in Oxford and second, that he knew I was going to be out in the Perkins Road woods that afternoon looking for a skeleton. That in turn means that he was probably in the courthouse when I was talking to James McAllister. We have a serial killer, and he is living right here in our midst, but his victims are from somewhere else. Not here."

Cobb looked at Will and said, "Will, I think you are probably right on all three counts. And I think that you will be safe by this time tomorrow. The fat is in the fire now, and our killer will know that by sometime tomorrow, if he doesn't already. The bodies have been found. Once he knows we have them, he will not have anything to gain by shooting you. Ed, let's keep him guarded for another, say, 48 hours and then see about removing coverage."

Jenkins turned to Will and said "One other question. Will, why didn't you go to medical school and become a doctor?"

"My parents died in a plane crash while I was in school. I didn't have the money for med school. The military would have sent me to med school, but then I would had to have careered in the military. As it was, I could get scholarships and assistantships for grad school, no strings attached."

All three agreed to call it a night and then meet back at the funeral home the next day around lunchtime.

CHAPTER TWENTY-FOUR

The state crime lab's pathologist was due in perhaps later that afternoon. Crime lab technicians were already working the woods where the bodies had been buried but so far had not found anything further. There might be more graves in the woods but no more depressions had thus far been found.

Cobb, Jenkins, and Will agreed that it was no longer necessary to protect Will from the shooter. TV crews from Atlanta had already interviewed Sheriff Cobb and they were running the story. Will could return to his regular classroom with the window shades up. Ed Jenkins even agreed to return Will's MG, though very reluctantly.

To Will, the most dramatic new revelation was that someone had entered the woods along the lower reaches of the creek and taken the still and its condenser. Cobb never admitted it, but both Will and Chief Jenkins always thought that Cobb had figured out or knew who the moonshiner was and let him recover his still in exchange for any information he might have about who else had been out in the woods.

Will's "expertise" as an anatomist was no longer needed. All three did, however, eat lunch together at least once a week. It started informally, and then it was by agreement in an effort to put together some leads.

No new leads were developed by those in the crime lab. The crime lab pathologist estimated that the oldest victim had been in the ground about 10 to 12 years. The most recent victim, the Negro, had been in the ground less than a year. He further confirmed all of Will's estimations as to age, cause of death and pregnancy of the victims.

Every week at lunch Jenkins, Cobb and Will put their heads together and tried to come up with something else to check out in hopes of developing a real lead. They checked local and nearby stores that carried rifle ammunition. Had any one made a purchase the day of the shooting? Had anyone working out on Perkins Road seen any vehicle out there that did not belong to a property owner or someone who worked for a property owner? They investigated all of the property owners of property on Perkins Road, as well as the people who worked for them. All the while, they knew it was only a matter of time, though, until there was another victim, and they might not even know about it unless somehow someone stumbled upon the body. It was very unlikely the shooter would dispose of a body in the Perkins Road woods again.

CHAPTER TWENTY-FIVE

Liza had, in the meantime, blended right into Oxford's daily life. She got a part-time job working in the library for Mildred Johnson and through the library began to make a nice circle of friends. Eleanor Herring introduced her into several local organizations, including Friends of the Library.

Every spring, Friends of the Library sponsored a tour of local homes. Oxford had a wide and well-earned reputation for having a substantial number of beautiful antebellum homes. Sherman had not visited Oxford on his infamous "march to the sea" in the fall of 1864. It was further east than his line of march had been.

Selecting the homes to be featured on the tour was a thankless task. Some homeowners did not want to deal with the hassle of having strangers traipsing through their houses over a two-weekend period. Other homeowners were demanding that their house be included on the tour, particularly if they were getting ready to list it for sale.

Liza was selected to head the tour committee for that year's tour. As the newest resident in Oxford, she had the fewest enemies and a fresh unbiased eye with which to select houses to be included.

Liza, it turned out, was an excellent choice. She added several new twists that injected new life into the long running project that had otherwise become a bit predictable over the years. Instead of just doing seven houses, she added five gardens to the tour. She also created several different packages, one package that included everything and was most expensive. One package included only gardens. Another package included five houses only and a package that included four houses and two gardens.

Several collateral events were also part of the tour weeks. Thursday night before the tour opened on Friday, there was a black-tie dinner for homeowners, garden owners, plus the guarantors backing the tour just in case. There were horticulture lectures, architecture lectures and luncheons on tour days. Each event was put together by a separate committee, and many ladies had served on the same committee for years—hence the wheel was not reinvented every year.

Several tasks, nevertheless, demanded Liza's personal attention. First and foremost of those tasks was selecting the houses for inclusion on the tour. She had borrowed the library's copy of the book written some years earlier on antebellum Oxford homes, Medora Field Perkerson's book *White Columns of Georgia*, plus several other books covering historic Georgia homes. The historic Oxford book provided a laundry list of potential houses with some discussion of each. However, the historic Georgia books provided a totally unanticipated benefit. It included Victorian houses, not just antebellum houses. Oxford's tours had theretofore always included only antebellum homes. Liza wanted to expand the scope of the tour to include a couple of Victorian houses, particularly in view of the fact that several Oxford Victorian houses were included in the Georgia books on significant historic houses.

Liza narrowed her list of "first choices" to the two Victorian houses that were considered architecturally significant in the Georgia books. One was owned by Calvin Perdue, president of Farmers and Merchants Bank. When she contacted Calvin, he readily and enthusiastically signed on. John Simpson owned the other house on her list of first choices. John was co-owner of a restaurant in the Buckhead part of Atlanta. Initially he said no. He just did not want to deal with the hassle of getting his house cleaned up and ready for the tour. In addition, he was seriously thinking of listing his house for sale and did not want the masses traipsing all over his grounds.

Liza was finally able to get him signed up, but only by assuring him that, first of all, no one would be allowed off the walkway going from the street into the house. Second, she would personally see to it that the inside of the house was spic and span before and at all times during the tour. But what finally closed the deal was that Liza convinced him that having had his house on the tour would have given it great exposure if he subsequently decided to list it for sale. In fact, she pointed out that was perhaps the most common reason people requested, even sometimes demanded, that their houses be included on the tour.

Getting ready for the tour had become more than a full time job. It was an all day and almost all night job. However, because it was sponsored by Friends of the Library and Oxford Public Library was its sole beneficiary, Mildred Johnson was very supportive of Liza's involvement.

About a week before the tour, Liza remembered her promise to John Simpson to get his house spic and span for the tour. She enlisted Rachel's help and Rachel, in turn, drafted her teenage daughter, Melody. On Saturday before the tour, all three loaded themselves and cleaning supplies into Liza's car and drove to

Simpson's house. Simpson had arranged to be gone to be out of the way as the women cleaned. Upon arriving, they noticed that Simpson had already done some cleaning. Several brown paper grocery bags filled to the brim with unwanted clothes and assorted items were stacked out back next to the garbage cans. Simpson had left a house key with Liza so they could get in. Only the first floor was to be open on the tour, which substantially lessened their task.

By end of the day, Simpson's downstairs was, indeed, "spic and span." The women were loading their supplies back into Liza's car when Rachel noticed a jar in Melody's hand. "What do you have in your hand, Melody?" Rachel asked.

"It's Apex Bergamot Hair Dressing," Melody explained. "I found it on top of one of the trash bags out on the back porch. Since it was in the trash, I didn't think anyone would mind. It is really top of the line and very expensive. Don't know why anyone would throw it away."

Rachel stated "It's probably OK this time, but in the future, ask someone first."

Then they left Simpson's and headed back to Carriage House where Rachel and Melody got in their car and went home.

Later that evening after Liza and Will had eaten supper, Liza suddenly, without any warning, jumped up and ran to the telephone. She got Rachel on the phone. "Rachel, you must know most, if not all, of the black maids who work in Oxford, right?"

"That I do," Rachel replied.

"Does John Simpson have a maid working for him?"

"No, ma'am. None that I have ever heard of. My understanding is that he is not around a lot. He is part owner of a restaurant in Atlanta and only comes to Oxford from time to time. He inherited that house from an old maid aunt ten or fifteen years ago. I think he has an apartment or condo or something in Atlanta. You know, those restaurant people work until late at night. It would be too hard for him to drive all of the way out here every night but he seemed to like having the house to get away too now and then."

"Thank you Rachel. Thank you. I'm sorry to have bothered you this late at night," Liza said and hung up.

"Will! I know who the serial killer is!"

CHAPTER TWENTY-SIX

"Will, it's got to be him. It all fits. The last victim was black. Rachel's daughter, Melody, found a jar of Apex Bergamot Hair Dressing in Simpson's trash this afternoon. Only a black female would have used that. Simpson is in the restaurant business in Atlanta. Restaurants are venerable clearing houses for young women runaways looking for a job. Most have no skill and little or no money. They are desperate. Believe me. I know. We used to see them all of the time at Hernando's, and we certainly weren't Atlanta or high end. Simpson would have a smorgasbord of young girls to choose from. If they got pregnant, he could just discard them. They would never be missed. No one would ever know."

Liza went on, "Since she had probably once been a runaway, he could just tell anyone that asked that she just moved on and no one would ever be the wiser. Will, it's got to be him."

"Liza, I think you may really be onto something," Will said when he could squeeze in a word.

"Will, get up. We have to go over to Simpson's house right now. There were grocery bags of clothes out back by the garbage cans.

I bet you a million dollars that those are women's clothes in those bags and if the crime lab people measure them and compare them to the sizes of the murdered victims, they will match at least one and maybe more of the dead girls. If we don't get those clothes before someone else does, we will have lost the evidence that opens up the entire case. Some girl's family might even be able to identify some of those clothes. Come on, Will. Let's go right now," Liza demanded. "Simpson may still be out of town. He left this morning before we got there to clean. I even have a house key. I bet we could find a rifle somewhere in his house."

Even Will was starting to believe. They picked up jackets and headed out. Liza drove her car since it was already out and she knew where Simpson lived.

They parked across the street from Simpson's house. Lights were on upstairs. Simpson was obviously back home.

"OK, Liza, what do we do now? Go home and come back later or wait?"

"We wait."

Will slid across the front seat and put his hand on Liza's thigh.

"I said we wait," she said. "We wait on that too."

Will pulled his hand back but did not move back across the seat. Then, a few minutes later he put his arm around her and moved even a little closer. Before she could push him away or even say anything, he gave her a soft lingering kiss.

"Will. You trying to get us arrested for indecent exposure or something. Get hold of yourself. No. That's not what I meant to say. Cool it until we get back home."

Will then asked her, "What are we going to do when we get the bags? If we take them, won't that warn him that someone is on to him?"

"Not really. As long as the bags are just sitting by the garbage cans, anyone might take them. If she had time, Melody would have probably gone through the bags this afternoon. As it was, she just took the pomade which was sitting at the top of one of the bags."

Finally, Simpson's upstairs lights went out. "We will give him about twenty or thirty minutes to get to sleep. Then we can go get the bags," Liza said.

About thirty minutes later, they quietly opened their car doors and slipped up Simpson's driveway to his trashcans. All four bags were gone. The grocery bags that had been there earlier that day were gone. Will gave Liza a questioning look. She looked around and then walked over to Simpson's car. It was too dark to see inside and the doors were locked.

She whispered to Will, "Wait a minute. I'll be right back," and headed back out the driveway to her car. She opened the glove box and got a flashlight, then eased back to Simpson's back yard. When she shinned the flashlight into the car, there they were. There were four brown paper grocery bags sitting on the back seat. She looked at Will and shrugged.

"We have got to leave them be," Will whispered. "It's one thing to take trash bags from around the garbage can. But it would be a felony for us to break into his car and take the bags even if we knew for sure that they contained clothes belonging to one of the murdered girls. It would also tip him off that something was afoot. Come on. Let's get out of here before we get caught."

When they got almost to the street, they saw an Oxford City police car parked directly behind Liza's. As Liza and Will approached their car, a policeman stepped out of the cruiser and shinned a flashlight on them.

Then a familiar voice said, "Professor, what the hell are you and Liza doing out here this time of night?" It was Kurt.

"Kurt," Will said, "If I tell you, it might poison some evidence in a very complicated criminal case. But what you can do and, in fact, must do, is keep an eye on that driveway. If that black Mercedes that is parked in back leaves, follow it without being detected. If Simpson throws out any brown paper grocery bags from his car, guard them. Don't let anyone near them. Call Ed or Cobb or me but guard them. If anybody gives you any trouble, explain to them that they are interfering with investigation of a criminal case and can and will be arrested if need be. This is probably that important, Kurt."

"Got it." Kurt replied. "And I thought that this was going to be another quiet, uneventful Saturday night in Oxford. Professor, you sure have a way of livening things up around here. One other thing, Professor. Whose car is this anyway? It has an Alabama tag."

"It's mine," Liza answered. "My sister drove it up here for me when she and my mother came up for the wedding. You met her at the reception, Kurt. I saw you two talking."

"No problem. Just had not seen it around. And don't forget to get a Georgia tag for it. And for that matter, don't forget to get a Georgia driver's license. You are a Georgia resident now."

"Let's get out of here before we attract attention," Will said.

Kurt moved his cruiser down the street and settled in for a long night.

CHAPTER TWENTY-SEVEN

Around nine o'clock Sunday morning the black Mercedes pulled out of the driveway and headed downtown. Eventually, it pulled into the Big Apple Super Market parking lot and drove around back to where the dumpsters were. Because it was Sunday, Big Apple was closed and street traffic was almost non-existent. Simpson got out of the car, opened the back door of his car, took the brown paper grocery bags out and tossed them into the dumpster. Then he drove away.

Kurt parked his cruiser in front of the dumpster and radioed dispatch to call Chief Jenkins and Sheriff Cobb and have them meet Professor Hampton at Big Apple Super Market parking lot right away. No lights. No siren. But right away. He also told dispatch to call Professor Hampton at home and tell him "that the deposit had been made" and tell him where.

Jenkins and Cobb arrived first. They were waiting when Will and Liza arrived moments later.

"Will, Liza—I know you would not drag us out here just to chit chat. What's going on?" Jenkins asked.

"I was just getting ready for church," Cobb said. "You got another body in there or something?"

Liza stepped in, "No new bodies, but maybe some critical evidence about one of the ones we already have. There are some brown paper grocery bags that Kurt just saw John Simpson throw in the dumpster. You need to get them out, and then let's take them to one or the other of your offices where we can go through them. Will and I believe that they may contain belongings of one or more of the murdered girls."

Liza then recounted Melody's finding and taking the jar of Apex Bergamot Hair Dressing, a product that would have been used only by a black female. She explained that after she got home, she started thinking about the hairdressing and wondered why John Simpson would have had it. Well, he wouldn't have. That was the point. But a young black girl staying with him might. If she were the last of the three murdered girls, she would have left it and probably her clothes and everything else behind.

Jenkins and Cobb flipped coins to see who climbed into the dumpster to get the bags. Jenkins lost so in he went. He handed the bags out to Cobb who loaded them into Jenkins' car. Then they all headed down to Jenkins' office.

Once there, they had a clerk take Kurt's statement about seeing Simpson discard the bags into the dumpster at Big Apple Super Market. Then they started removing, numbering and photographing each and every article in each bag.

After several hours and numerous articles of men's clothing, they had not discovered anything of real interest. But when they started on the third bag, their luck changed.

There were numerous articles of women's clothing including bras, panties, blouses, pants, costume jewelry and makeup of the type often used by blacks. There was also an all but empty jar of Apex Bergamot Hair Dressing buried down in the bag. Jenkins immediately went out to his dispatcher's desk and told her to call the state crime lab and have them to get a crew ready to work new evidence relating to the three serial murders near Oxford.

Perhaps most interesting, also in bag three, there were several pairs of black slacks and white blouses of the sort often worn by waitresses in restaurants. In the fourth bag, they found shoes, belts and a few small purses.

All four had missed both breakfast and lunch, and suppertime was quickly approaching. Jenkins smelled like the inside of the Big Apple Super Market dumpster filled with old produce discarded the evening before. At first, they talked about meeting for supper somewhere after Jenkins had a chance to cleanup. Will suggested John Simpson's restaurant in Atlanta, which drew glares until the others realized he was only joking. Then it was suggested that eating together might draw unwanted attention and questions. Then Cobb suggested that he and Jenkins have their wives join them and all three couples meet for supper. Even if they talked some shop during supper, their wives were used to keeping silent about police business. An hour later, they were being seated at Oxford Club for an early supper.   .

Oxford Club could always be counted on for very good food and top-notch service. It was only open Wednesday through Sunday, which, because it was the closest Oxford could offer in the way of fine dining, meant that, when it was open, it was always crowded. Initially, it started out as a gentlemen's club. However, once husbands died, many wives wanted to continue membership privileges and by-laws were amended accordingly.

Immediately upon being seated, Frances Jenkins imposed ground rule number one, no shoptalk. In an effort to implement that ground rule, Frances asked Liza how things were coming together for the upcoming Tour of Homes. Liza replied that the tour was coming together nicely until yesterday when she identified one of the tour home owners, John Simpson, as the serial killer. After that, there was little talk of anything else. So much for ground rule number one.

Liza explained that she did not feel threatened by Simpson. They would be in contact, of course, but how was she going to look him in the eye without having it written all over her face that she knew he was a murderer? But then, if she evaded him, would that make him suspicious? It was finally agreed that she needed to appoint a liaison for each of the homeowners since she could not be everywhere once the tour got underway.

CHAPTER TWENTY-EIGHT

Thursday evening's gathering of guarantors, home and garden owners with property on the tour plus the tour committee went off without a hitch. John Simpson attended. Immediately upon arriving, he sought out Liza and thanked her for the splendid cleaning done on his house. Liza thanked him very sincerely for allowing his house on the tour. Ticket sales were already almost double their previous best year, an increase being attributed to including homes other than just antebellum homes, and Simpson's home was one of the two non-antebellum homes on the tour. In retrospect, Simpson said he felt guilty having them clean his house for the event. He offered to reimburse Liza whatever expense she had incurred on his account. When she graciously refused reimbursement, he insisted on offering free meals at his restaurant to those who had cleaned his house. Liza didn't tell him it was her, Rachel and Rachel's teenage daughter. About that time, another homeowner joined Liza and Simpson. Liza made introductions and gradually moved on as the new acquaintances got to know each other. Liza took note of one fact. Simpson was not wearing a wedding ring and did not have a date.

Liza was up early first thing Saturday, making a last minute check of the houses and gardens on the tour and double-checking that all personnel were on duty as planned. She walked through the downstairs of Simpson's house. Everything was as they had left it after the previous Saturday's cleaning. Then, on an impulse, Liza headed up the stairs to the second floor. The tour guide already stationed at the house asked her what in the world she was doing. Only the ground floor was on the tour and the stairs were corded off. As Liza headed up the stairs she said something to the effect that she just wanted to see what the upstairs was like.

There were two front bedrooms connected by a bathroom and two back bedrooms also connected by a bathroom. Liza went to the front bedrooms first. One of the front bedrooms had been lighted last Saturday night when she and Will had attempted to retrieve the garbage bags from out back. One front bedroom was unused. The other was obviously Simpson's. His tux from Thursday night's gala was still draped over the back of a chair. Liza wasn't sure what she expected but a quick search did not turn up anything the least bit suspicious.

She then went to the two back bedrooms. One of them was obviously unused for a long time although the other bedroom showed signs of recent occupancy. The bed had been slept in and the covers only pulled up. There were some clothes in the dresser though not many. There were some clothes hanging in the closet, and leaning in the back corner of the closet was a Marlin 30/30 lever action rifle. On the shelf above the rifle were several boxes of ammunition for the rifle. One was all but empty.

Without hesitating for even a moment, Liza picked up the rifle and chambered a round. She walked over to the bed and tightly rolled up a pillow. She stuck the end of the barrel of the rifle deep into the pillow. Even with the pillow, it made a hell of a racket. The bullet went through the pillow, through the mattress and into the floor. Liza ejected the shell casing from the rifle, picked it up and returned the rifle to the closet where she found it. She could not recover the bullet but it was probably too damaged to reveal anything anyway.

By this time, the tour guide downstairs was frantically calling Liza's name and asking what was wrong.

Liza calmly walked back down the stairs and told the tour guide, "You did not hear anything or see anything because nothing happened." Whereupon she walked out the front door, got in her car and drove off.

She drove straight to Chief Jenkins' office. Fortunately, Jenkins was there. Liza gave him the shell casing, explained how she came by it and asked if it could be compared to those retrieved from the farm out on Perkins Road.

"Damn straight," Jenkins said as he dropped the casing into an evidence bag, sealed it and labeled it. "Kurt or R.T. will take it to the crime lab in Atlanta first thing Monday morning. Liza, you've dug up more evidence in this case than all of the rest of us combined. Your talents are being wasted in that library."

Liza smiled, gave him a quick peck on the cheek, thanked him and headed back to the tour.

CHAPTER TWENTY-NINE

Apparently, the shell casing awakened some interest in personnel at the crime lab. Tuesday afternoon results from comparing Liza's shell casing with those found at the Perkin's Road farm were in. All were fired by the same rifle. They were a perfect match. Also included was a report on the clothing Simpson had thrown away Sunday morning a week ago. Hairs contained in the recovered hairbrush belonged to a Negro and they matched perfectly the hair from the last victim buried out on Perkins Road.

Chief Jenkins immediately called Sheriff Cobb and insisted that he needed to come right over. It looked like they may have their serial killer.

Jenkins and Cobb sat down together and started discussing what to do next. Both readily agreed that they needed to get a warrant for Simpson's arrest and started Jenkins' secretary typing up the papers. They called the courthouse to find if any of the judges were in the building. There was. Judge McDow was hearing routine motions. Jenkins told the clerk not to let him leave. They had urgent business to bring before him very shortly.

"OK," Cobb said. "What next? Even if we have Simpson's arrest warrant hand delivered to Atlanta, no telling when they might get around to actually picking him up, even though it is a murder warrant."

"Wait a minute. I have an idea," Jenkins said. He then told his secretary to find the new attorney in town, James McAllister, and ask him to get over here as soon as possible. "It's an emergency."

Literally, moments later, McAllister was ushered into Jenkins office by R.T.

McAllister looked at Cobb and Jenkins, then said, "I'm not sure if I'm under arrest or not. R.T. saw me walking from the courthouse back to my office and told me to get in his car. When I asked him what it was about, he said he didn't know but he was going to bring me here one way or the other. What's up?"

"Mr. McAllister. If I'm not mistaken, the law firm you were with in Atlanta included the county attorneys for Atlanta, Fulton County, Georgia," Jenkins said.

"Yes, sir. They were and are."

Jenkins continued, "We need your expertise on a technical point of law. Now don't give me any crap about you'll check on it and get back to me. Tell me now or get on that phone and call someone in your old firm to get an answer. Can a sheriff of one county in Georgia lawfully execute a felony arrest warrant in any and all other counties of Georgia or is his jurisdiction limited to the county where he holds office?"

"No problem," Mc Allister replied. "All Georgia sheriffs and their deputies have statewide jurisdiction. Now as a practical matter, professional courtesy dictates that visiting sheriffs who are going to execute a warrant outside of their home county at least give a heads up to the sheriff whose county they are going to act in. Come on now. What's up? This sounds like pretty serious stuff for Oxford, Georgia."

"Thank you, James. You have advanced the cause of justice greatly. We'll keep you posted. R.T. will run you back wherever you need to go," Jenkins said.

Cobb then turned to Jenkins and said, "Ed, let's go eat supper at Mr. Simpson's fancy restaurant in Atlanta. Since we will be on official business, we'll let the county pick up the tab."

"What about giving Fulton County a heads up?" Jenkins asked.

"When we get through eating and are ready to execute the warrant." Cobb replied. "Then and only then."

CHAPTER THIRTY

John Simpson had both an Atlanta business address and phone number and an Atlanta home phone number and address on file with Oxford Police Dept. in the event that anything happened at his Oxford house while he was in Atlanta. Cobb and Jenkins got in Cobb's car and headed to John Simpson's restaurant in Buckhead, the affluent suburb of north side Atlanta.

Once there, they were seated by the hostess and given menus. Each ordered the best the menu had to offer and then began to enjoy a scrumptious meal. While they were eating, John Simpson arrived at their table and welcomed them. He sat down with them and ultimately asked what brought them to Buckhead.

Cobb explained that they were in town on official business and had decided to drop in while they were in town. Cobb said Simpson could probably help them out a bit when they finished supper, which was as good as they had hoped it would be.

As they finished their dessert, John Simpson magically reappeared at their table and asked, "How can I be of help—other than picking up your tab?"

Cobb asked, "Is there somewhere a little more private where we might can talk?"

"Sure, in my office" Simpson said as he lead the way down a hall past restrooms to a private office. "What can I do?"

"John," Jenkins began, "you have undoubtedly heard about the three bodies of murdered young women found out on Perkins Road. And no doubt you know that someone shot at Professor Hampton when he was out there looking around."

Jenkins continued. "We have positively identified the rifle that fired at Professor Hampton as the 30/30 lever action Marlin in the upstairs bedroom of your Oxford house."

"What the hell!" Simpson exclaimed.

"There is more," Jenkins said. "Let me finish before you say anything. Sunday morning before the Tour of Homes, you took four brown grocery bags of miscellaneous clothes and threw them in the dumpster at Big Apple. Two of the bags contained clothes and personal effects belonging to the most recent murder victim, a young Negro girl who was pregnant, we believe, by her murderer. Now all that is pretty circumstantial, admittedly, but I have to tell you we have a warrant for your arrest for her murder. You no doubt know you have a right to a lawyer, and you don't have to tell us anything."

"First," Simpson said, "You have got the wrong guy. Now I know that is what they all say, but you do. From what you have told me, I know who you are really looking for—John Clayborn, my former business partner in this restaurant.

"John was my partner in this restaurant for over 15 years, from the time we moved from downtown out here to Buckhead. He had a key to my Oxford house and sometimes spent time out there with one of his girlfriends. John frequently formed liaisons with young girls that worked in the restaurant. What you really need to know is that the girl before his current fling was Negro. She was a runaway from somewhere in South Carolina. I'm sure I still have her employment information in our files.

"John," Jenkins continued, "I need to remind you that you were the one who one of my officers saw taking the trash bags and throwing them into the dumpster at the Big Apple."

"That's obviously true. I did." Simpson replied. "With the tour of homes coming up and my house on the tour, I took that opportunity to do some spring cleaning through out the house, even including the upstairs which was not going to be on the tour. I even asked Clayborn to clean out the upstairs rooms that he sometimes used. He did and left the trash bags on the back porch, not having any idea about where to put them to be picked up. I took them to the Big Apple dumpster because there was no guarantee that they would be picked up from out front on the curb before the tour of homes started Thursday."

"But what you really need to know," Simpson continued, "is that yesterday I finished buying John Clayborn out. He is, right now, on his way to somewhere in Florida where he intends to start a new restaurant, although he had not fully decided on where when he left."

"When did he leave?" Cobb asked.

"Last night, or more probably, first thing this morning."

"How was he traveling?

"He drives a late model black Cadillac and he will have a young blond girl with him that worked as a waitress here until yesterday."

Cobb looked at Jenkins. "Ed, I think we were about to arrest the wrong guy, what do you think?"

"Looks that way to me too."

"Fellows, let me add one more thing," Simpson said. "Please keep this between ourselves, but I don't date girls. I never have. I have never had sex with a girl. I just keep pretty much to myself because I just don't want a lot of complications.

"Ed, if he gets to Florida, we'll ultimately get him back, but we'll play hell finding him first. Any ideas?"

"John, can I borrow your Atlanta phone book and then use your phone?" Jenkins asked.

"Sure, have at it."

Jenkins dialed the number for the Georgia State Patrol. "This is Ed Jenkins, Police Chief of Oxford, Georgia. Seated next to me is Sheriff Cobb also of Oxford. We have a serial murder suspect driving down probably U S Highway 441 to Florida. If there is any way to stop and take him into custody, it will save us a lot of time and Georgia taxpayers a lot of money. Can you help us? I can get you the arrest warrant in less than an hour but we may not have that much time before he gets into Florida."

"Chief, get the warrant to our headquarters on Confederate Ave as soon as you possibly can. In the meantime I'll just say I am pretty sure that we can work something out."

Jenkins then called his office and asked dispatch which deputies were on duty. "Both Kurt and R.T." she said.

"Get them in immediately. Get a blank warrant and type it up exactly as the John Simpson warrant only put in the name John Clayborn. Get them to get it signed by the judge ASAP and then rush it to Georgia Highway Patrol Headquarters on Confederate Avenue in Atlanta, using red lights and siren all the way."

CHAPTER THIRTY-ONE

L ewis Johnson had been a State Trooper for over 20 years. He was an old hand and thought he had seen just about everything law enforcement officers see and had done just about everything law enforcement officers do. It was another boring Tuesday night on US Highway 441. He was parked on the shoulder of the highway when his radio came to life.

"Attention all units in South Georgia District Four. Attention all units in South Georgia District Four. Locate and intercept a late model black Cadillac occupied by one John Clayborn and a young, blond female before it crosses into Florida. Clayborn is a serial murderer but may not know that an arrest warrant has been issued for his arrest. Approach using caution. He is dangerous and may be armed. Take him in custody using any means necessary. Call for backup if needed and notify this office upon spotting him. Do not allow him out of your possession at any time or for any reason once he is in custody. His license tag number follows."

Johnson turned back into Highway 441 and headed north and away from the Florida State Line. He wanted to get more working room to pursue Clayborn before the Florida line in event Clayborn showed up. About twenty miles back up Highway 441, Johnson swung his car around and parked on the southbound shoulder of Highway 441. Traffic was pretty light. Several speeders passed but Johnson let them go. His luck, he would be ticketing a speeder and Clayborn would get by.

By about 10:30 Johnson started thinking. "If I had a young blond female in the car with me I would not be driving all night. I would find me a motel to spend the night in and pretty early on." Again, he eased back into Highway 441 and headed north this time all of the way into Fargo, Ga. There were only a few motels in Fargo and all were on Highway 441. Johnson carefully checked all of the cars in the parking lots of every Fargo motel. There were no black Cadillacs.

If they were off the highway and in this part of the state, there was only one other place they could be. They had to be in a rental cabin in Stephen Foster State Park inside the Okefenokee Swamp. That presented two problems. First, it would leave Highway 441 open to the Florida State Line. Second, the park locked the gate at 7:30 PM every night. And it was 15 miles from the gate to the cabins inside the park.

Johnson got on his radio to his area supervisor and explained his hunch. His supervisor checked. There was another patrol car stationed 35 miles north of Fargo on Highway 441. No black Cadillac had passed him since the alert went out. If Clayborn had passed that trooper before the alert went out, he would have passed Johnson before now or he was holed up for the night. It was also unlikely that Clayborn was on any side road since he had no reason to suspect that he was being hunted.

Johnson's supervisor instructed Johnson to gain access to the park and check for the black Cadillac. After waking up several motel clerks in Fargo, Johnson finally found one who knew where the park ranger lived that locked and unlocked the park gate each night and morning. Johnson found his residence and banged on the door until lights came on and the park ranger came to the door.

Johnson explained that it was very likely that a serial murderer was staying in the park but that needed to be verified. The Ranger finished dressing, got the gate keys and headed out the door.

Johnson stopped him. "Don't they issue you any artillery?" he asked. "Yes sir, but only for emergencies."

"Then go get all that you got. This is what it's for," Johnson explained.

Together they entered the park and drove the 15 miles to the cabin area of the park. All 20 cabins were along one winding road. As they passed the third cabin, they saw the black Cadillac parked out front. They were already driving slowly enough that they could verify the tag number without further slowing down and perhaps attracting attention.

Once they got away from Clayborn's cabin, Johnson tried to raise his supervisor again. No luck. Inside the park, Johnson's radio was out of range.

Johnson turned to the park ranger. "How in the hell do you communicate with the outside world from in here?" he asked.

"There is a telephone inside the boat rental office, but I don't have a key," he said.

Johnson swung his car around and headed for the main gate. They were going to go back and open it in any event if Johnson's supervisor decided to send back up. At 90 mph, they were back at the main gate in less than ten minutes.

Johnson raised his supervisor who then notified headquarters in Atlanta that Clayborn had been located.

It was decided to send in two additional units as backups.

Once back in the cabin area, they instructed occupants of the cabins near Clayborn's to remain inside until they were told otherwise, no exceptions. They were told that a rabid raccoon had been spotted nearby.

Even though they were as quiet as possible, Clayborn apparently heard some activity and came out on his side porch.

Thinking fast, the park ranger asked him to stay inside until they gave an all clear. They had spotted what they were pretty sure was a rabid raccoon near the garbage cans next door and were trying to locate it. They did not want any guests to accidently come into contact with it. Even healthy raccoons were very aggressive. Rabid ones were very unpredictable. Clayborn went back inside and locked his door.

Next, they had to devise a plan to separate Clayborn from his girlfriend. Last thing they wanted was a hostage situation.

About 30 minutes after telling Clayborn about the rabid raccoon, the park ranger went into the nearby woods and fired a single shot into the ground.

Johnson, in the meantime, had let the air out of one of Clayborn's back tires. When Clayborn came back out on his porch, he hailed the park ranger and asked if they had gotten the rabid raccoon.

"Yep, we are pretty sure we did, but it looks like you have a flat tire."

Clayborn walked down the steps and headed for his car. One trooper came from around the back of the cabin and blocked the cabin door. The park ranger and Johnson immediately took Clayborn into custody and handcuffed him. Johnson then brought up his patrol car and placed Clayborn in the back seat.

The young woman with Clayborn came running out of the cabin demanding to know what was going on. When told that Clayton was under arrest, she demanded that she be allowed to go with him wherever he was being taken. She stated that, even though they were not actually married, they were living together and she was pregnant with their child.

One of the Troopers began removing the flat tire on Clayborn's car and replacing it with the spare. He explained to the young woman that he did not know where Clayborn was being taken but that she could follow him to the park entrance where he could radio dispatch and then let her know.

With Clayborn secure in the back of his patrol car, Johnson drove to the entrance of the park and radioed dispatch that Clayborn was in custody. He was told to deliver Clayborn to Sheriff Cobb in Oxford, Georgia, as soon as possible. He was also told that when he passed through Folkston, Georgia, he could pick up another trooper to share driving with. Upon receiving the prisoner, Sheriff Cobb would have arranged for both troopers to get some well-earned sleep and breakfast before they had to return to South Georgia

CHAPTER THIRTY-TWO

S heriff Cobb was immediately notified that Clayborn had been arrested and would be delivered to Oxford around 8:00 AM or 9:00 AM. At 8:00 AM, Cobb, Chief Jenkins and the District Attorney, Tom Thackston, met in Cobb's conference room. It was time to dot I's and cross T's. They had an arrest in a very high profile case. Clayborn would undoubtedly hire a lawyer. They could not afford any stupid mistakes.

Thackston spoke first. "Sheriff Cobb, I understand that you had to act fast and I congratulate you on your fast work. At this point, we only have a very circumstantial murder case against Clayborn for the murder of the young black girl. Based on what John Simpson has told you, we can link her and Clayborn together and we can link Clayborn to the rifle used to shoot at Professor Hampton out on Perkins Road. Simpson needs to get us the girl's name and identity here ASAP. With that, I can get Clayborn indicted but we will need more evidence to actually convict him. But indictment will be a start. The fact that he was arrested on his way out of Georgia will make it hard for him to get bond. He is too high a risk to flee in what is obviously a major crime and probably a series of murders."

Cobb turned to Chief Jenkins. "Ed, can you get with John Simpson and get identification of the young black girl first and then any of the others that can be linked to Clayborn. Call Tom with the black girl's name so he can go to the Grand Jury, hopefully this morning."

"Tom," Cobb continued, "Can you get the Grand Jury in this morning?"

"Damn right. For this case, I'll have them back in by 10:00 this morning. I could probably get a quorum over at Henri's Bakery right now."

Thackston continued. "Based on John Simpson's testimony and the Crime Lab report, I also intend to get Clayborn indicted on attempted murder of Professor Hampton. The more we throw at this guy, the more likely some of it will stick. Based on Simpson's statement, we know the rifle used to shoot at Hampton was Clayborn's. We may even be able to match his fingerprints to prints on the brass shell casing recovered at the scene. I don't know how long fingerprints last or if any were recovered when the shell casings were recovered out on Perkins Road last January. Cobb, you'll need to follow up on that."

Jenkins and Thackston headed out on their respective missions. Cobb went to a phone and called Will Hampton. "Professor, if you have a minute, can you come by my office. Quite a lot has happened in the last 24 hours."

"On my way right now," Will replied.

Will joined Sheriff Cobb in Cobb's office and got a rundown of events beginning with identification of the shell casing recovered by Liza from the rifle now known to be Clayborn's with those recovered out on Perkins Road after the shooting. "At this point it's all circumstantial but its starting to connect up in a pretty good chain," Cobb said.

As Cobb and Will started walking out of Cobb's office, Trooper Johnson brought Clayborn handcuffed through the front door.

Will grabbed Cobb by the arm and pulled him back in to the private office.

"Sheriff, I know that man. Well, I don't really know him but he was in the Tax Commissioner's office last January, the morning I was looking through the records trying to identify the owner of the property out on Perkins Road. He was there buying a car tag when McAllister accused me of invading his legal domain, and I explained why I was there and what I was looking for."

"Will, that was almost six months ago. Why would you possibly recognize him now?" Cobb asked.

"Sheriff, he was wearing the best looking Harris Tweed sport coat that I ever saw. It was herringbone woven from dark brown mixed with light brown and tan. He was wearing dark brown flannel slacks, white shirt with a black paisley wool necktie. His clothes were tailored to perfection. I bet you a million dollars you will find that outfit hanging in his closet today."

"Will, I betting you are right. Gladys, see if you can get Tom Thackston back over here right now and tell him to bring a court reported. We are also going to need a search warrant for Clayborn's car and residence. Will, we'll need you to testify before the Grand Jury a little later this morning so we can get Clayborn indicted for trying to kill you. In the meantime, stay here in my office, if you don't mind. I have a guest to welcome."

With that, Sheriff Cobb walked out of his private office and introduced himself to both Trooper Johnson and Clayborn.

"Mr. Clayborn, you are under arrest for the murder of an as yet un-named black female and attempted murder of Professor William Hampton. You do not need to say anything at this point. As soon as you are processed, you will be allowed to make any telephone calls you need to."

Cobb then turned to his deputy, "Process him and lock him up."

He then turned back to Trooper Johnson and stuck out his hand. "Trooper, I want to thank you and congratulate you for the outstanding work you and those who worked with you did last night in capturing Mr. Clayborn. There is a bakery up the street on the right. Go have breakfast, and I'll call and tell them to hold the tab for me. I can offer you sleeping quarters here but I'm quite sure you will be much more comfortable at the motel next to the college. You passed it on your way into town. They are expecting you and I'll of course take care of the bill. Thank you again very, very much. And before you go back to South Georgia, please come back by here and give me the details about last night."

Within thirty minutes or so, Tom Thackston, the DA, arrived with a court reporter. Thackston first interviewed Will, then swore him in and questioned him under oath. Thackston explained that taking down Will's testimony under oath was really just a precaution. He would be needed to appear and testify before the grand jury as soon as they were convened which should be about anytime now. He also asked Will to get Liza so she could testify about finding Clayborn's rifle and recovering the shell casing from it.

As Thackston was leaving Cobb's office, a tall slender blond girl walked in the front door. "I want to see John Clayborn. I understand that he was brought here sometime early this morning."

Cobb stepped forward and introduced himself. He went on and explained that Clayborn was being charged with the murder of his most recent girlfriend and attempted murder of Professor William Hampton. "In fact," Cobb asked, "didn't you tell Trooper Johnson that you are pregnant with Clayborn's child?"

"That's correct," she stated. "He is very excited about becoming a father. It will be his first child. We are in the process of moving to Florida but were stopped last night at the Okefenokee Swamp so he could show it to me. He said it is very beautiful even in winter and it is one of his favorite places to visit. We were going to rent a boat and explore the swamp today."

"Young lady," Cobb said, "I have every reason to believe that you would not have left the Swamp alive. I believe you would have been strangled and your corpse hidden in some remote part of the swamp never to be found except perhaps by an alligator."

"That's impossible," she cried out. "You are wrong. This whole thing is a big mistake," she exclaimed.

Cobb took her into his private office and outlined where matters stood. As he concluded, he asked her if Clayborn's clothes and effects were still in his car. They were. He then asked if he could look through them and the car. If necessary he would get a search warrant, but with her permission, the warrant would not be necessary. She consented and Cobb borrowed her car keys and opened the car's trunk. Behind the suitcases in the trunk was a lever action 30/30 rifle that Cobb immediately seized. Among the clothes in a travel clothes bag was a herringbone tweed sport coat that matched Will's description perfectly, together with a pair of dark brown flannel slacks. Cobb also seized them as well.

Clayborn's girlfriend was completely devastated. When she finally got some control of herself, Cobb recommended that she call John Simpson and ask for her job back, at least until she could sort out her plans. Simpson not only rehired her immediately, but also suggested that she get Cobb or one of his deputies to take her to his house in Oxford until he could pick her up.

Cobb noticed that, when she collected her clothes and effects from the car, she also took a fat envelope from the glove compartment. Cobb assumed that it was cash but did not say anything. If cash, she was going to need all of the help she could get in the very near future. One of the deputies then drove her to John Simpson's Oxford house. Of course, she knew where the extra house key was hidden and was able to let herself inside.

Before the morning was over, Will, Liza and John Simpson had testified before the grand jury, and the grand jury had returned true bills against John Clayborn for attempted murder of Professor William Hampton and for the murder of one Ella Matthews, a 20-year-old Negro female.

Will returned to his office in Science Hall where he completed grading finals and posting grades. Once again, Dean Herring locked down the campus, this time to protect Will from the press. To avoid the press, Will left his car on campus and walked home after leaving unnoticed through a side gate. Liza had taken time off after doing the Tour of Homes, and Mrs. Calhoun had thoughtfully closed and locked the gates to the estate.

CHAPTER THIRTY-THREE

Will had elected not to teach summer school. Instead, he and Liza quietly packed the car late that evening and eased out of Braxton Hall and Oxford for an extended trip. Liza had acquired a serious interest in southern antiques along with an extensive knowledge of southern homes. First stop on the trip was Charleston, South Carolina, where Will was able to show her where he had gone to college, The Citadel, and to visit with several of his favorite professors and mentors—Metcalf in Biology, Wideman in Chemistry, Doyle and Achurch in English, Reves in Math and Herring in Electrical Engineering. Will never took engineering but Col. Herring lived next door to Will's advisor, Col. Metcalf, and through that contact, they became close friends as well.

Will and Liza were also able to visit with and spend considerable time with Milby Burton, Director of the Charleston Museum. Will's parents had been friends with the Burtons so, when Will went to The Citadel, he was immediately included into the Burton family. Milby Burton was widely known as an ornithologist and as co-author of a standard text on southern birds. However, he was equally expert on southern antique furniture and had published the standard reference on Charleston furniture and furniture makers. Will and Liza spent over a week viewing the Museum's antique furniture collection plus the public and private homes of Charleston.

After a week in Charleston, Will and Liza drove to Winston Salem, North Carolina, and the Museum of Early Southern Decorative Arts. MESDA, as it was called, was created by and out of the antique collection of Frank Horton and his mother. Milby Burton and Frank Horton were best friends so when Liza and Will arrived at MESDA, Horton was waiting for them and saw to it that they had all of the best that the Museum could offer.

From MESDA, Will and Liza drove to Williamsburg. Frank Horton had called ahead and, once again, the red carpet was awaiting their arrival. At Williamsburg, they stayed in one of the restored Williamsburg houses and spent a week exploring the town and both the public and private collections of antique American furniture. Will was able to spend a day in the Hay Shop where furniture reproductions were made using 18th century tools and techniques. He was also allowed in the blacksmith's shop where many of the tools were actually made.

Winterthur in Delaware, home of the antique furniture collection amassed by Henry DuPont, was their final destination. At Winterthur, they did not attempt to see the entire collection but toured displays of a couple of periods. By the second day at Winterthur, they were saturated with furniture and headed back home via the Blue Ridge Parkway.

CHAPTER THIRTY-FOUR

Upon returning home and getting a good night's sleep, Will was up bright and early the next morning as was his habit. He picked up the stack of accumulated mail and started thumbing through the envelopes. One stood out. It was about six inches square. It was hand addressed in beautiful script to both Will and Liza and had an Oxford return address that Will did not immediately recognize. Upon opening the envelope, Will was amazed to find the wedding announcement of John Simpson and a lady's name he did not recognize, Ellen Davison. In addition to the wedding announcement, there was an invitation to a reception at the couple's home, but it had already taken place before Liza and Will had returned to Oxford.

Will walked back into the bedroom where Liza was still asleep. "Liza, John Simpson got married week before last. We were invited to a reception at his house. I thought you said he wasn't the marrying type."

Liza rolled over, thought a minute and then said,"Ed Jenkins told me that John told both him and Cobb that he was either gay or asexual. They weren't sure which because of the rather ambiguous way he stated it. Oh well, best wishes to them," and she rolled back over.

Will returned to the kitchen to refresh his coffee, picked up the phone and called Ed Jenkins who he knew was also an early riser.

"Ed, Liza and I got back last night. Going through the accumulated mail, I found John Simpson's wedding announcement. What's the deal? I thought you said he wasn't…"

Before Will could finish the sentence, Ed interrupted and started explaining. "Will, Ellen, his bride, is the very beautiful blonde that John Clayborn had with him when he was arrested at Stephen Foster State Park. Cobb and I believed then, and are still convinced now, that Clayborn planned to strangle her and dump the body somewhere in the swamp. She was and is pregnant by Clayborn. Everybody pretty much knows that Clayborn is not going to be around to help raise or contribute to the support his child. Ellen had been a great waitress at the restaurant so when she returned, Simpson let her stay at his house and gave her, her job back. Apparently, it is one of those situations where one thing led to another or perhaps it is just a marriage of convenience. She was faced with raising a child alone and on a modest income at best. John, on the other hand, whatever his sexual proclivity might be, now has instant respectability. He has a wife and is about to be a father. Ellen now has a husband capable of providing a good home for her and the child. Actually, very few here in Oxford will know that John is not the biological father. She is not even showing yet. But you know, I don't think John and Ellen would even care if the whole world knew. They are just that comfortable with the arrangement."

"Well, I'll be damned, Ed. But, like Liza said, 'best wishes to them.'"

After Will hung up, he headed outside to begin catching up on yard work at Braxton Hall. About a week later, he was in his office looking over his fall semester schedule when his phone rang. It was Ned Conway in Caseville.

"Will, I hardly know where to begin. Connie spent most of the summer here with me. She was driving back to Chattanooga last night and was hit head-on by a drunk driver. She is and has been on life support since she arrived at the hospital. She will die when they cut it off."

Will interrupted, "Ned, I can't tell you how sorry I am. Is there anything I can do?"

"Let me finish, Will. There is more. Connie is pregnant. She is almost full term. When it became apparent that she was pregnant, she told me that you are the father. Now don't say anything. Just listen to me for a minute. Connie was 41 last December when you were up here. She was very much aware that her biological clock was winding down. She did not want to leave me without an heir, and there were no prospects in her foreseeable future. When she heard about the cave disaster on the news, she came home that night to be with me if needed. Once she got here, she realized you were staying at the house. She also realized that her timing for ovulation was probably right and she acted. I guess you know the rest better than me.

"Doctors at the hospital are confident that they can take the baby by C-section and that it will survive and be healthy. I know I am throwing a lot at you. Would you be willing to take the child and raise him or her? At my age, I just can't but I'll do everything I can to help support my grandchild. It will also be a great comfort knowing that the child is being raised in a good home, which I know you and your wife will provide. My old friend, Ed Jenkins, has told me that your wife is a wonderful girl."

"Ned, I'm stunned. Since last December, I have gotten married but even without talking to my wife, Liza, I'm sure we will head for Chattanooga immediately and will provide the best home we can for my child."

"Look, Will, I know you have a great future but I also know professors don't make a lot of money. There will be a recovery from the drunk driver, and then there will be my estate, which, though not huge, is not exactly modest either. There is also life insurance on Connie's life through the school system where she was teaching and, because her death will be ruled accidental, the insurance will pay double indemnity. But right now, the most immediate matter is delivery of the baby. Doctors are ready to do the C-section as soon as you can be here, if you will come. Then they will take Connie off life support."

"Ned, I need to talk to Liza of course, but I'm sure we'll be there first thing in the morning. Tell me where we need to be."

"Oh, and Will. Connie and I already have on hand just about everything you are going to need for the baby—diapers, crib, blankets. The hospital will give you a starter supply of formula."

Will closed his office and headed to Carriage House. "Liza, you remember I told you about the Scouts killed in the Northwest Georgia cave. Initially many thought Ned Conway had caused the explosion that killed the Scouts. He didn't and we became good friends when I proved that he was uninvolved. In fact, he made that chestnut bowl on the bookcase and gave me the chestnut blocks in my woodshop. I have just found out from Ned about a chapter in that story that I did not know about..."

After only a moment's silence, Liza said, "Let's pack right now and leave as quick as we can. If we leave right away, we can get most of the way to Chattanooga tonight, maybe even all of the way. That way we will be fresh in the morning. We need to take my car. There's barely enough room for two in your MG. No way it could handle three even one being a baby. "

Will and Liza found Ned Conway at the hospital. When they saw each other, they embraced without saying a word, tears streaming down their faces. Ned Conway then turned to Liza and said, "Thank you. Thank you. You are obviously every bit as wonderful as Ed Jenkins said you are."

While they were awaiting delivery of the baby Ned invited, no insisted, that Will, Liza and the baby stay with him for a few days.

It was a girl. Will, Liza and the baby left the hospital for Ned's house. Ned stayed behind to be with Connie until the end.

Connie's funeral was two days later. All of Caseville turned out, and she was laid to rest next to her mother in the church cemetery. Will left that afternoon for Oxford to start fall semester's classes. Liza and the baby, whom they named Connie, stayed with Ned until Will could return the following weekend, which he did.

By the time Liza and baby Connie arrived in Oxford, Herring, Calhoun & Company were already in high gear. At the outset when the story broke, there was a brief discussion about what propriety might demand. It was immediately agreed, propriety be damned. Will, Liza and now Connie were "one of them" and that Oxford would do anything and everything it could to support the new family. Showers were arranged. Eleanor Herring coordinated purchase of clothes. Edna Calhoun coordinated purchase of food. Friends of the Library created a wish list for "everything else."

Liza took a week off from the library. When she returned to the library, she either took Connie with her and set up her crib in the employee workroom or she got Rachel's daughter, Melody, to stay with her at home.

CHAPTER THIRTY-FIVE

W ill walked into his office after his 9:00 AM class. Sitting there, waiting on him, were Ed Jenkins, Sheriff Cobb and Tom Thackston, the District Attorney. Jenkins spoke first.

"New developments, Will. Clayborn, through his attorney, has offered to plead guilty to murdering the two young women found near the still as well as shooting at you. However, he denies having anything to do with a third murder. In a nutshell, it doesn't make any sense unless he is telling the truth."

Tom Thackston then spoke up. "Under Georgia Law, he can't get the death sentence if he pleads guilty which he would very likely get if he went to trial. He will undoubtedly get life in prison but again under Georgia Law, he would be eligible for parole after seven years. Now, as a practical matter, he would not be paroled after seven years. That just never happens. But whether he killed two women or three women would not make that much difference in a parole hearing. He simply has no reason to claim innocence as to the third murder unless he is in fact telling the truth. And if he is telling the truth, and I for one believe he is, then we have an unsolved murder on our hands."

Will then asked the obvious question, "What's this got to do with me? He has no reason to come after me again even if or when he gets paroled."

Cobb was sitting in Will's chair behind his desk fiddling with the Megalodon Shark's tooth on the desk. He leaned forward and said, "Will, the three of us worked together so well last time, we thought we might try it again. In particular, we need your expertise in re-examining the pathology reports, maybe even all of us going out to the gravesite and re-examining it for whatever might have been overlooked. Remember, my deputies stumbled upon that third grave about dark. It wasn't anywhere near the graves down by the still. It was up near the top of the hill near the road. And it was after dark by the time they actually dug and found the body."

Tom Thackston spoke up. "It seems we are in agreement that Clayborn committed two murders and that he shot at Will and that there is no objection to letting him plead guilty to just those three offenses. I'll notify Clayborn's attorney that we have a deal. Gentlemen, let me know when you solve the third murder. In the meantime, congratulations on the splendid work so far," whereupon Thackston got up and excused himself.

No one spoke for a moment. Then Will said, "Suits hell out of me. I don't have any classes or labs this afternoon. Weather out on Perkins Road has to be perfect for digging in the woods. Let's go give it a shot."

As he went down the hall, Will ducked into the geology supply room and picked up several sieves, then drove to Carriage House where he changed into digging clothes. Driving up Perkins Road past the fallen-in Williams homestead, he saw sheriff and police cars parked up ahead on the side of the road near the top of the hill. Once there, it was obvious where the others had gone into the woods. Will parked his car and followed their path into the woods. He quickly came upon the group standing around what had obviously been the third grave. Much of the excavated dirt had been shoveled back into the grave or had washed back into the hole by rains.

Will distributed the sieves to the deputies, and they first began sifting the dirt that remained outside of the grave. Nothing of interest was recovered so they moved to the grave itself. After sifting about a foot or so of dirt, they began to recover small fragments of rotted cloth, then a few buttons and then finally a silk label with the name "J.P. Allen."

Will immediately spoke up. "J.P. Allen is one of the high-end ladies clothing stores in Atlanta. They have two stores, one in the heart of downtown Atlanta and one on East Paces Ferry Road in the heart of Buckhead. My mother used to shop there some. If you think these cloth fragments are remnants of the victim's dress and she was from around here, I know who can identify her, Margaret Clark. Margaret has worked at J.P. Allen forever. She always waited on my mother. She will be able to tell us who in this area shopped at J.P. Allen. Everyone that shopped there used a store charge account. Nobody ever paid cash or wrote a check for merchandise. I bet Margaret will be able to tell us not only who bought the dress but when they bought it, its size, stock number and what they paid for it."

There was a moment of silence while all that Will had said sunk in. Finally, Sheriff Cobb spoke up and said, "I'll be damned. Will, the ball's in your court now. Go see Margaret whatever-her-name-is."

Out of an abundance of caution, the deputies continued sifting dirt from the grave but nothing else was recovered.

It was too late in the day for Will to get to J.P. Allen's before it closed and he was giving weekly Friday tests to his classes the next day. All agreed that time was not necessarily of the essence, but they all wanted to know the identity of the victim as soon as possible. They all also agreed that it was critical that no word leak out that Clayborn didn't kill all three girls. All three men then went to Dean Herring's office and asked if, for reasons undisclosed, the Dean would administer the tests to Will's classes the next day. Dean Herring immediately agreed and then, to everybody's amusement, quoted Sherlock Holmes by saying "and the game is on," but of course having no idea what the game was.

CHAPTER THIRTY-SIX

Margaret Clark recognized Will the moment he stepped through the front door of J.P. Allen. She stepped out from behind the counter, crossed the sale floor and gave him a big hug.

"Will, Will, Will. Haven't seen you since your parents' funeral. We all miss them so much. And I saw you on television about those Scouts killed in that cave up near Chattanooga. But enough. What brings you here?"

Margaret and Will went through the names of J. P. Allen's Oxford customers. Ten or twelve years ago, there was only one 20-year-old customer from Oxford—Missy Perdue, daughter of Calvin Perdue, owner of Farmers and Merchants Bank. And she had bought a wrap Thanksgiving weekend 1949 while home from college for Thanksgiving. The wrap was rather exotic but that was typical of Missy. She was always quite avant-garde. Will swore Margaret to secrecy and hoped she would be good to her word.

Will was back in Oxford before lunch and joined Jenkins and Cobb for lunch at Henri's. Both men said "Oh shit" at the same time as soon as Will told them what Margaret Clark had told him. Will was mystified by their reactions.

Cobb then spoke up. "Will, you have no idea how bad this is. We all know that the girl was pregnant. While you were in Atlanta, Ed and I contacted the State Crime Lab and asked them to blood type the fetus and to give us any additional information that might help us identify the victim. They had already typed the blood of both the victim and the fetus, which they gave us. They also advised us that the child the victim was carrying was racially mixed, Negro and white, which of course means that the father of the child Missy was carrying was Negro."

Jenkins then stated that no rape of a white woman or white girl had been reported in the area in recent memory, especially one involving someone like Missy Perdue. "What the hell. Only thing I can figure is that she had a Negro lover off at college."

"We need to find out a lot more about Missy Perdue," Will said, "and I know just where to start—Edna Calhoun. She knows everything about everybody in Oxford. And again, we can't let it out where we are with this."

After lunch, Will headed to Carriage House. Mrs. Calhoun's car wasn't in her garage, so she obviously wasn't back in town yet, but she would be by morning though. It was Rachel's Saturday to clean.

Saturday morning, Will climbed the back steps to Edna Calhoun's kitchen, knocked and entered. "Mrs. Calhoun, I need your help. You know everything that there is to know about people in Oxford. Sheriff Cobb and Chief Jenkins need some information about a prominent former resident of Oxford. I'm going to have to give you some very sensitive confidential information, and it involves an on-going murder investigation. Please, please, please don't breathe a word to anyone about anything I'm about to ask you."

"Well, it obviously involves the murders of those young women by that restaurant man. I'm afraid I don't know anything about any of them."

"Mrs. Calhoun, what can you tell me about Missy Perdue? Who were her friends? Who did she date around here? Who did she run with?"

"Will, she left here years ago. She and her father had some sort of falling out. Her mother had died of cancer a year or so before. She went back to college her senior year, graduated I understand, and moved to New York where I guess she is today. She never comes home any more. Her father goes to New York now and then and sees her. That's about all I know. She was always very head strong, swimming against the flow, so to speak. Spoiled if you ask me. Poor little rich girl that got everything she ever wanted but never got enough spankings. Smoked in high school. Had a sports car and always drove way over the speed limit. Wrecked a couple of them but always escaped unhurt. Does that help any?"

"Mrs. Calhoun, you obviously know Mr. Simpson's former business partner, Clayborn, is charged with murdering the three pregnant young women that were found buried out on the Williams property on Perkins Road. Actually, he only murdered two of the three. The third murder is totally unrelated to the two committed by Clayborn. The third woman was Missy Perdue and yes, she was pregnant. What's more, she was pregnant by a Negro man. Rape does not seem to have been involved. Could she have been involved with anyone from around here or do you think it was someone from where she was in college?"

"Will, I'm speechless. She went to Middleton College for women in Charlottesville, Va. I would imagine that it's pretty conservative. It's not like she went to some university in California or New York. She taught swimming to children at the city pool as part of the summer program. Never remember her dating anyone in particular from around here. I don't think she had any close girlfriends either. Probably thought nobody around here was good enough."

Rachel, who was washing breakfast dishes over at the sink, chimed in. "She briefly had something going on with one fellow from around here, Johnson Williams. He worked maintenance for the city, which included working at the city swimming pool. That's where they sort of got acquainted. He was very handsome, a war veteran and he was Negro. She was just a bored little rich girl."

Both Mrs. Calhoun and Will were speechless. Finally, Will spoke up. "Where's he now? How can we get in touch with him?"

"He's dead. Shot in the back. Just over ten years ago. Thanksgiving, 1949. In our own front yard."

"Rachel, did you say in 'our own front yard?' "

"Yes. Johnson was my younger brother. I was married and working in the school cafeteria when Johnson came back from World War II. My husband, Clifford, worked maintenance for the city. Still does. He is the one that got Johnson on with the city. Johnson lived at our place on Perkins Road with our father and worked the place evenings and on weekends. I wasn't living there by then. Clifford and I rented a place in town. It was Thanksgiving weekend. Late in the evening, right at dark. Dad was in the house. Johnson was outside finishing whatever he was working on. There was a pistol shot. Dad ran out of the house. Johnson was lying face down in the yard near the road. He had been shot in the back and was dead."

"Did anyone call the sheriff?" Will asked in disbelief.

"Professor, you don't understand. Nobody was going to do anything about a Negro who got shot, particularly if it got out that he had had something to do with a white girl. Clifford and I went over to the house and helped my dad dig a grave. We buried Johnson along where my mother is buried, my grandfather and all of the other Williams. My father is buried out there now. Like I said, back then nobody would have cared. Law was only for white people. Only time law applied to black people was if a white wanted it to. Things are some better now with Sheriff Cobb and Chief Jenkins being the law. But back then, it would have just caused a whole lot trouble if we had said anything about Johnson being shot, especially since he had to have been shot by a white. It would have been ruled self-defense or something, even though he was unarmed and was shot in the back in his own front yard."

"Rachel, I don't know what to say. There's nothing I can say except that Sheriff Cobb and Chief Jenkins are investigating Missy Perdue's murder, and I'm sure they will put just as much effort into finding your brother's killer even at this late date. In fact, I need to go bring them up to date. Please, neither of you breathe a word of any of this to anyone. There is one and maybe two killers out there. We can't afford to do anything that might tip them off that that we know all three victims found out on Perkins Road weren't killed by Clayborn."

Thirty minutes later Cobb, Jenkins and Hampton were sitting in Cobb's office with the door closed. Will had brought them up to date.

After a long silence, Cobb finally said what all three had to be thinking. "Calvin Perdue has got to be our prime suspect for both murders. He either did them or had them done. At this point, we only have circumstantial evidence though. I'm going back out to Perkins Road one more time and this time to look for Johnson's corpse. We ought to be able to recover a bullet at least. Ed, you and Will knock off for the rest of the weekend and think of a next move. Will, what's your schedule like Monday?"

"Out of class at 10:00 and until 1:30."

"OK, back here at 10:15 Monday with fresh ideas. I'm going to Perkins Road."

CHAPTER THIRTY-SEVEN

Will was the last to arrive in Sheriff Cobb's office Monday morning, but Cobb and Jenkins had been busy. Jenkins had called the Registrar at Middleton College. Their records indicated Missy Perdue did not return to the college after Thanksgiving break 1949. Her father had called to say that she was not coming back but that she was going to work with him at his bank. He was shorthanded since his wife died and really needed some good help.

Cobb had gone to the Williams farm Saturday afternoon and recovered a .38 caliber bullet from Johnson's body. He also noted that the dorsal rib at T-3 was shattered, consistent with Johnson having been shot in the back.

Will had also been busy over the weekend. He had called Rachel to see if she knew Johnson's blood type. She still had his World War II dog tag with his blood type stamped into it. It was the very rare AB type—so rare that only about 4%, white or black, have it. From the Crime Lab pathology report, Will found that Missy Perdue's fetus also had AB. Missy was type O, the most common blood type.

Cobb or Jenkins finally said, "Perhaps it's time we when to the bank and had a chat with Calvin Perdue."

CHAPTER THIRTY-EIGHT

Sheriff Cobb and Chief Jenkins went into the lobby of Oxford Farmers and Merchants Bank. Calvin Perdue, seeing them approach, stood up, extended his hand as gregariously as ever and said, "Gentlemen. To what do I owe this honor?"

Jenkins took the extended hand and asked, "Calvin, might we have a few minutes, maybe in your private office?"

"By all means. Come this way."

Once seated across the desk from Perdue, Cobb spoke first. "Calvin, we have identified with certainty, your daughter Missy's body. It was buried, as we think you know, out on the Williams's property on Perkins Road. We also know and think you know that she was pregnant, and from comparison of blood types, we are almost certain that Johnson Williams was the baby's father. Both baby and father have AB blood type. It is a very rare blood type. Only 4% of the white or black population have AB. Missy had type O, the most common. We have recovered a .38 caliber slug from Johnson's body, and we know that Missy and Johnson were both killed over Thanksgiving weekend 1949. We know that Missy never went back to Middleton College after Thanksgiving vacation 1949. Middleton has told us that you notified the college she was not going to return. Instead, she was going to start helping you in the bank, which we all know she did not do. Now admittedly, all of this is pretty circumstantial but it is very persuasive to us. We believe either you killed both individuals or you had them killed. You don't have say anything, but if you have a better explanation of what we know, now might be a good time to let us have it."

Calvin leaned forward and put his elbows on the desk and his face in his hands. He did not speak. Then, as he sat back up, he opened the top drawer of his desk and with one quick, smooth movement removed a .38 caliber snub-nosed revolver, put it to his temple and shot himself before Jenkins or Cobb could say or do anything.

Chief Jenkins jumped up and went out into the bank lobby. There were no customers present. He announced to the employees that Mr. Perdue had just taken his own life and the details would be made public shortly. Chief Jenkins further explained that no banking irregularities were involved but that it involved a family matter. He then instructed the head cashier to lock the front door and to close the bank. All employees were then told to leave the bank and go home until there was an announcement about re-opening the bank.

Will had remained in Cobb's office when Cobb and Jenkins went to interview Calvin Perdue. He first heard about the shooting when Cobb telephoned his office for dispatch to send the coroner over to the bank because Perdue had shot himself. Will immediately called Liza, told her what had apparently happened and suggested that she come over to Sheriff Cobb's office. Moments later Liza appeared with Connie in arms. About the same time Sheriff

Cobb's wife and Chief Jenkins' wife appeared. Will had no idea how they found out that something was afoot. They all moved into the conference room. Will was only able to fill them in up to the decision to go visit Calvin Perdue.

It was about an hour before Cobb and Jenkins returned to the office. Cobb immediately gave his staff a quick rundown of recent events, and then he and Jenkins joined the others in the conference room. Jenkins, Cobb and Will each reiterated their findings that lead to the decision to visit Calvin Perdue. Cobb and Jenkins then explained what transpired once they met with Perdue.

At first, no one could say a word. Then Liza spoke up. "There is at least one loose end remaining. Rachel needs to be told." Looking at Sheriff Cobb and Chief Jenkins, she said, "And it might be best coming from one of you before she hears no-telling-what from no-telling-who."

Jenkins immediately picked up a local phone book, looked up the cafeteria's number at Oxford Elementary and dialed. With Rachel on the phone, Jenkins began explaining. "Rachel, we now have more information about your brother Johnson's murder. If you can come down to Sheriff Cobb's office, we can bring you up to date. I can send one of my deputies over to the school and give you a ride over here."

"I will get my husband, Clifford, to bring me down. If people see me riding in a police car, they will think I've done something."

When Rachel and Clifford arrived, Cobb and Jenkins took them into Cobb's private office.

Cobb spoke first. "Rachel, Calvin Perdue killed both his own daughter, Missy, and your brother Johnson. Missy was pregnant with Johnson's child. Calvin apparently found out when Missy returned from Middleton College in Virginia for Thanksgiving vacation. Lots of circumstantial evidence came together, all of which left us with only that conclusion. Chief Jenkins and I went to the bank a little while ago and confronted Calvin with all of the evidence we had gathered. He never said a word but reached into his desk drawer, took out a pistol and committed suicide right there in front of us."

Clifford put his arms around Rachel's shoulders and held her close. She was silent for a few moments, then there was a quiet sob, then another and followed by others.

Chief Jenkins reached over and took Rachel's hand. "Rachel, we would never have solved Johnson's and Missy's murders without your help. You gave Professor Hampton the key information that connected everything together. We are very much indebted to you for your helping us."

"One other thing that you might want to think about. Johnson was a veteran with an outstanding war record. His remains can be removed to a National Cemetery and interred with full military honors at no expense to you. On the other hand, if you wish him to remain buried in the family plot on Perkins Road, an appropriate head stone can be placed at his grave again at no cost to you and a funeral conducted with full military honors. Think about it. We can talk about it later, anytime you are ready."

Cobb and Jenkins left Rachel and Clifford alone in Cobb's private office and re-joined the others in the conference room. No one seemed in any particular hurry to leave. About that time, one of Cobb's clerks leaned in the door to say that she was going down to Henri's to pick up the staff's lunch order. Did anyone want anything from Henri's?

They all did and were waiting on their lunch orders when Liza once again spoke up. "This entire business is like something out of a Greek play. First, a white girl and her Negro lover are murdered by her father because she is carrying her Negro lover's child. Then a Negro girl is murdered by her white lover because she is carrying his child. And to make the circle complete, a white girl is murdered because she is carrying a white child. In any event, Calvin Perdue's and John Clayborn's evil deeds did at last come home to roost. Justice may have slept but only for a while."

CHAPTER THIRTY-NINE

A week later, Will had just finished his Embryology lecture when, as he started down the hall from his classroom to his office, the Science Department secretary ran out of her office calling, "Dr. Hampton, Dr. Hampton. Lawyer Troutman is on the phone and says he must speak to you immediately. It's an emergency."

Will stepped into the department office and picked up the phone, but before he could say more than hello, Troutman was saying, "Dr. Hampton, this is Edward Troutman. I urgently need your services once again. There has been an explosion..."

Made in the USA
Monee, IL
31 May 2021